Evelyn Everett-Green

Monica

A Novel. Vol. 3

Evelyn Everett-Green

Monica
A Novel. Vol. 3

ISBN/EAN: 9783337092023

Printed in Europe, USA, Canada, Australia, Japan

Cover: Foto ©Andreas Hilbeck / pixelio.de

More available books at **www.hansebooks.com**

MONICA.

MONICA.

A Novel.

BY

EVELYN EVERETT-GREEN.

Author of
"TORWOOD'S TRUST," "THE LAST OF THE DACRES,"
" RUTHVEN OF RUTHVEN," ETC,

IN THREE VOLUMES.

VOL. III.

LONDON:
WARD AND DOWNEY,
12, YORK STREET, COVENT GARDEN, W.C.
1889.

PRINTED BY
KELLY AND CO., GATE STREET, LINCOLN'S INN FIELDS,
AND KINGSTON-ON-THAMES.

CONTENTS.

CHAPTER THE THIRTIETH.

CHAPTER THE THIRTY-FIRST.

CHAPTER THE THIRTY-SECOND.

MONICA.

MONICA.

CHAPTER THE TWENTY-THIRD.

BEATRICE.

" BEATRICE, I believe my words are coming true, after all. I begin to think you are getting tired of Trevlyn already."

It was Monica who spoke thus. She had surprised Beatrice alone in the boudoir at dusk one afternoon, sitting in an attitude of listless dejection, with the undoubted brightness of unshed tears in her eyes.

But the girl looked up quickly, trying to regain all her usual animation, though the attempt was not a marked success, and

Monica sat down beside her, and laid one hand upon hers in a sort of mute caress.

"You are not happy with us, Beatrice, I see it more and more plainly every day. You have grown pale since you came here, and your spirits vary every hour, but they do not improve, and you are often sad. I think Trevlyn cannot suit you. I think I shall have to prescribe change of air and scene, and a meeting later on in some other place."

Monica spoke with a sort of grave gentleness, that indicated a tenderness she could not well express more clearly. For answer, Beatrice suddenly flung herself on her knees before her hostess, burying her face in her hands.

"Oh, don't send me away, Monica! Don't send me away! I could not bear it—

indeed I could not! I am miserable—I am wretched company. I don't wonder you are tired of me; but ah! don't send me away from you, and from Trevlyn. I think I shall *die* if you do. Oh, why is the world such a hard, cruel place?"

Monica was startled at this sudden outburst, for since the day following her arrival Beatrice had showed herself unusually reserved. She had been *distraite*, absorbed, fitful in her moods, but never once expansive; therefore, this unexpected impulse towards confidence was the more surprising.

"Beatrice," she said gently, "I did not mean to distress you. You know how very, very welcome you are to stay with us. But you are unhappy; you are far more unhappy than when you came."

Beatrice shook her head vehemently at this point, but Monica continued in the same quiet way. " You are unhappy, you are restless and miserable. Beatrice, answer me frankly, would you be happy if Tom Pendrill were not here? He has already outstayed his original time, and we could quite easily get rid of him if his presence is a trouble to you. We never stand on ceremony with Tom, and Randolph could manage it in a moment."

Beatrice lifted a pale, startled face.

"Tom Pendrill?" she repeated, almost sharply. " What has he got to do with it? What makes you bring in his name? What do you know about—about——?" She stopped suddenly.

" I know nothing except what I see for myself—nothing but what your face and his tell me. It is easy to see that you have known each other before, and under rather exceptional circumstances, perhaps. Do you think it escapes me, that feverish gaiety of yours whenever he is near — gaiety that is expended in laughing, chatting, flirting, perhaps, with the other guests, but is never by any chance directed to him? Do you think I do not notice how quickly that affectation of high spirits evaporates when he is gone; how many fits of sad musing follow in its wake? How is it you two never talk to one another? never exchange anything beyond the most frigid commonplaces? It is not your way to be so distant and so cool, Beatrice. There must be a reason. Tell me truly, would you not be happier if Tom Pendrill were to go back to St. Maws?"

But Beatrice shook her head again, and heaved a long, shuddering sigh.

"Oh, no, no!" she said. "Don't send him away. Nothing really matters now; nothing can do either good or harm. Let him stay. I think his heart is made of ice. He does not care; why should I? It is nothing but my folly and weakness, only it brings it all back so bitterly—all my pride, and self-will, and stubbornness. Well, I have suffered for it now."

It was plain that a confession was hovering on Beatrice's lips; that she was anxious at last to unburden herself of her secret. Monica helped her by asking a direct question.

"Were you engaged to him once?"

"No—no! not quite. I had not got quite so far as that. I might have

been. He asked me to be his wife, and I—
I——" She paused, and then went on
more coherently.

"I will tell you all about it. It was
years ago, when I was barely eighteen—a
gay, giddy girl, just 'out,' full of fun, very
wild and saucy, and thoroughly spoiled by
persistent petting and indulgence. I was
the only daughter of the house, and
believed that Lady Beatrice Wentworth
was a being of vast importance. Well, I
suppose people spoiled us because we were
orphans. We were all more or less spoiled,
and I think it was the ruin of my eldest
brother. He was at Oxford at the time I
am speaking of ; and I was taken to Com-
memoration by some gay friends of
ours, who had brothers and sons at
Oxford.

"It was there I met Tom Pendrill. He was the 'chum' of one of the under-graduate sons of my chaperon, and he was a great man just then. He had distinguished himself tremendously in the schools, I know—had taken a double-first, or something, and other things beside. He was quite a lion in his own set, and I heard an immense deal in his praise, and was tremendously impressed, quite convinced that there was not such another man in the world. He was almost always in our party, and he took a great deal of notice of me. He gave us breakfast in his rooms, and I sat next him, and helped to do the honours of the table. You can't think how proud I was at being singled out by him, how delighted I was to walk by his side, listening to his words of wisdom, how elevated I often felt, how taken out of myself into quite a new world of thought and feeling."

Beatrice paused. A smile — half sad, half bitter—played for a moment over her face ; then she took up the thread of her narrative.

" I need not go into the subject of my feelings. I was very young, and all the glamour of youth and inexperience was upon me. I had never, in all my life, come across a man in the least like him—so clever, so witty, so cultured, and withal with so strong a personality. He was not silent and cynical, as he is now, but full of life and sparkle, of brilliance and humour. I was dazzled and captivated. I believed there had never been such a man in the world before. He was my ideal, my hero ; and he seemed to court me, which was the most wonderful thing of all.

" You know what young girls are like ? No, perhaps you don't, and I will avoid generalities, and speak only of myself. Just because he captivated me so much— my fancy, my intellect, my heart—just because I began to feel his power growing so strongly upon me, I grew shy, frightened, restive. I was very wilful and capricious. I wanted him to admire me, and I was proud that he seemed to do so ; but I did not in the least want to acknowledge his power over me. I was frightened at it. I tried to ignore it—to keep it off.

" So, in a kind of foolish defiance and mistrust of myself, I began flirting tremendously with a silly young marquis, whom I heartily despised and disliked. I only favoured him when Tom Pendrill was present, for I wanted to make him jealous, and to feel my power over him. Coquetry is born in some women, I believe; I am sure it was born in me. I did not mean any harm. I never cared a bit for the creature. I cared for no one but the man I affected now to be tired of. But rumours got about. I suppose it would have been a very good match for me. People said I was going to marry the cub, and I only laughed when I heard the report. I was young, vain, and foolish enough to feel rather flattered than otherwise."

She paused a moment, with another of those bitter-sweet smiles, and went on very quietly:

" Why are girls so badly brought up?

I was not bad at heart; but I was vain and frivolous. I loved to inflict pain of a kind upon others, till I played once too often with edge-tools, and have suffered for it ever since. Of course, Tom Pendrill heard these reports, and, of course, they angered him deeply; for I had given him every encouragement. He did not know the complex workings of a woman's heart, her wild struggles for supremacy before she can be content to yield herself up for ever a willing sacrifice. He did not understand; how should he? I did not either till it was too late.

"I saw him once more alone. We were walking by the river one moonlight night. He was unlike himself—silent, moody, imperious. All of a sudden it burst out. He asked me almost fiercely if I would be his wife—he almost claimed my promise as his right—said that I owed him that reparation for destroying his peace of mind. How my heart leapt as I heard those words. A torrent of love seemed to surge over me. I was terrified at the depth of feeling he had stirred up. I struggled with a sort of fury against being carried away by it, against betraying myself too unreservedly. I don't remember what I said; I was terribly agitated. I believe in my confusion and bewilderment I said something disgusting about my rank and his—the difference between us. Then he cast that odious marquis in my teeth, supposed that the report he had heard was true, that I was going to sell myself for the reversion of a ducal coronet, since I thought so much of *rank*. I was furious;

all the more furious because I had brought it on myself, though, had he but known it, it was ungenerous to take me at a disadvantage, and cast my words back at me like that—words spoken without the least consideration or intention. But, right or wrong, he did it, and I answered back with more vehemence than before. I don't know what I said, but it was enough for him, at any rate. He turned upon me—I think he almost cursed me—not in words, but in the cruel scorn expressed in his face and in his voice. Ah! it hurts me even now. Then he left me without another word, without a sign or sound of farewell —left me standing alone by that river. I never saw him again till we met in your drawing-room that night."

Beatrice paused; Monica had taken her

hand in token of sympathy, but she did not speak.

" Of course, at first I thought he would come back. I never dreamed he would believe I had really led him on, only to reject him with contempt, when once he dared to speak his heart to me. We had quarrelled; and I was very miserable, knowing how foolish I had been ; but I never, never believed for a moment that he would take that quarrel as final.

" Two wretched days of suspense followed. Then I heard that he had left Oxford the morning after our interview by the river, and I knew that all was over between us. That is the story of my life, Monica ; it does not sound much to tell, but it means a good deal to me. I have never loved anyone else—I do not think I ever shall."

Monica was silent.

" Neither has he."

Beatrice's eyes were full of a sort of wistful sadness and tender regret ; but she only kissed Monica very quietly, and stole silently from the room.

CHAPTER THE TWENTY-FOURTH.

" Ah, Randolph! I am glad you are in. It is going to be such a rough night!"

Monica was sitting by the fire in her own room, waiting for her husband to join her there, as he always did immediately upon coming in from his day's sport. They had one or two more guests at Trevlyn now— men, friends of Randolph's in days past; but nothing ever hindered him from devoting this one hour before dinner to his wife. It was to Monica the happiest hour of the day.

" I am so glad to have you safe back. Are you not very wet?"

"No; I was well protected from the
rain; but it has been a disagreeable sort
of day. The other fellows were carried off
to dine at Hartland's. We came across
their party just outside the park, and he
begged us all to accept his hospitality for
the night, as the weather was getting so
bad. Haddon and I came home to tell
you, but the rest accepted the invitation.
We shall be quite a small party to-night."

Monica looked up with a smile.

"I think I am glad of that, Randolph."

He sat down and put his arm about her.

"Tired of our guests already, Monica?"

"I don't know—-I like to have your
friends, and to help to make them enjoy
themselves; but I don't think there is any
such happiness as having you all to
myself."

He held her closer to him, and looked with a proud fond smile into her face.

" You feel that too, Monica ? "

" Ah, yes ! How could I help it ? "

He fancied she spoke sadly, and would know why.

"I think I have been sad all day," she answered ; "I am often sad before a storm, when I hear the wind moaning round the house. It makes me think of the brave men at sea, and their wives waiting for them at home."

There was a little quiver in her voice as she spoke the last words. Randolph heard it, and held her very close to him.

" It is not such a very bad night, Monica."

" No; but it makes me think. When you are away, I cannot help feeling sad, often. Ah, my husband! how can I tell you all that you have been to me these happy, happy months?"

"My sweet wife!" he murmured, softly.

"And other wives love their husbands," she went on in the same dreamy way, "and they see them go away over the dark sea, never to come back any more," and she shivered.

"Let us go to the music-room, Monica," said Randolph. "You shall play the hymn for those at sea."

He knew the power of music to soothe her, when these strange moods of sadness and fear came upon her. They went to the organ together, and before half-an-hour had passed Monica was her own calm, serene self again.

"Monica," said Randolph, "can you sing

something to me now—now that we are quite alone together? Do you remember that little sad, sweet song you sang the night before I went away to Scotland? Will you sing it to me now? I have so often wanted to hear it again."

Monica gave him one quick glance, and struck the preliminary chords softly and dreamily.

Wonderfully rich and sweet her voice sounded ; but low-toned and deep, with a subtle searching sweetness that spoke straight to the heart :

> " ' And if thou wilt, remember—
> And if thou wilt, forget.' "

There was the least little quiver in her voice as it died into silence. Randolph bent over her and kissed her on the lips.

" Thank you," he said. " It is a haunting little song in its sad sweetness. Somehow, it seems like you, Monica."

But she made no answer, for at that moment a sound reached their ears that made them both start, listening intently. Monica's face grew white to the lips.

The sound was repeated with greater distinctness.

"A gun!" said Randolph.

"A ship in distress!" whispered Monica.

A ship in distress upon that cruel, iron-bound coast—a pitch-dark night and a rising gale!

Randolph looked grave and resolute.

"We must see what can be done," he said.

Monica's face was very pale, but as resolute as her husband's.

"I will go with you!" she said.

He glanced at her, but he did not say her nay.

In the hall servants were gathering in visible excitement. Lord Haddon was there, and Beatrice. The distressing signals from the doomed vessel were urging their imperative message upon every heart. Faces were flushed with excitement. Every eye was turned upon the master of the house.

" Haddon," he said, " there is not a man on the place that can ride like you, and you know every inch of the country by this time. Will you do this?—take the fastest, surest horse in the stable, and gallop to the nearest life-boat station. You know where it is ?—Good ! Give the alarm there, and get all in readiness. If the ship is past our help, and drifts with the wind, they may be able to save her crew still."

Haddon stayed to ask no more. He was off for the stables almost before the words had left Randolph's lips.

Monica was wrapping herself up in her warm ulster ; Beatrice followed her example ; the one was flushed, the other pale, but both were bent on the same object—they must go down to the shore to see what was done. They could not rest with the sound of those terrible guns ringing in their ears.

The night was pitchy black, the sky was obscured by a thick bank of cloud. The wind blew fierce and strong, what sailors would call " half a gale." It was a wild, " dirty " night, but not nearly so bad a one as they often knew upon that coast.

The lanterns lighted them down the steep cliff-path, every foot of which, however, was well known to Monica. She kept close beside her husband. He gave her his hand over every difficult piece of the road, Beatrice followed a little more slowly. At last they all stood together upon the rocky floor of the bay.

Monica looked out to sea. She was the first to realise what had happened.

"She has struck on the reef!" she said. "She does not drift. She has struck!"

"And in such a sea she will be dashed to pieces in a very short time," said Randolph, as another signal flashed out from the doomed vessel.

Other lights were moving about the shore. It was plain that the whole population of the little hamlet had gathered at the water's edge. Through the gusts of rain they could see indistinctly moving figures; they could catch as a faint murmur the loud, eager tones of their voices.

"Stay here, Monica," said Randolph, "under the shelter of this rock. I must go and see what is being done. Wait here for me."

She had held fast by his arm till now! but she loosed his clasp as she heard these words.

"You will come back?" she said, striving to speak calmly and steadily.

"Yes, as soon as I can. I must see what can be done. There seems to be a boat. I must go and see if it cannot be launched. The sea in the bay is not so very wild."

Randolph was gone already. Beatrice and Monica were left standing in the lee of a projection of the cliff. They thought they were quite alone. They did not see a crouching figure not many paces away, squeezed into a dark fissure of the rock. The night was too obscure to see anything, save where the flashing lights illumined the gloom. Even the wild beast glitter of a pair of fierce eyes watching intently passed unseen and unheeded.

Monica looked out to sea with a strange fixed yearning in her dark eyes. She was looking towards the vessel, struck fast upon the very rock where she had once stood face to face with death. How well she remembered that moment and the strange calmness that possessed her! She never realised the peril she was in—it had seemed a small thing to her then whether she lived or died. She recalled her feelings so well—was she really the same Monica who had stood so calmly there whilst the waves leaped up as if to devour her? Where was her old, calm indifference now?—that strange courage prompted by the want of natural love for life?

A sense of revelation swept over Monica at that moment. She had never really feared, because she had never truly loved. It was not death even now that she dreaded for herself, or for her husband, but separation. Danger, even to death, shared with him, would be almost welcome: but to think of his facing danger alone— that was too terrible. She pressed her hands closely together. It seemed as if her very soul cried to Heaven to keep

away this dire necessity. Why she suspected its existence she could not have
explained, but the shadow that had hung
upon her all day seemed wrapping itself
about her like a cloud.

" Monica, how you tremble ! " said
Beatrice. " Are you cold? Are you
afraid ? "

She was trembling herself, but it was
with excitement and impatience.

Monica did not answer, and Beatrice
moved a little away. She was too restless
to stand still.

Monica did not miss her. A storm was
sweeping over her soul—one of those
storms that only perhaps come once in a
life-time, and that leave indelible traces
behind them. It seemed to her as if all
her life long she had been waiting for this

hour—as if everything in her past life had
been but leading up to it.

Had she not known from her earliest
childhood that some day this beautiful,
terrible, pitiless sea was to do her some
deadly injury—to wreck her life and leave
her desolate ?   Ay she had known   it
always—and now—had the hour come ?

Not in articulate words did Monica ask
this question.   It came as a sort of voice-
less cry from the depths of her heart.   She
did not think, she did not reason—she only
stood quite still, her hands closely clasped,
her white face turned towards the sea, with
a mute, stricken look of pain that yet expressed but a tithe of the bitter pain at her
heart.

But during those few minutes, that
seemed a life-time to her, the battle had

been fought out and the victory won. The old calmness had come back to her. She had not faced this hour all her life to be a coward now.

She was a Trevlyn—and when had a Trevlyn ever been known to shrink or falter before a call of duty?

Beatrice rushed back with the greatest excitement of manner.

"They have a boat, but nearly all the men are away—the strong men who could man it easily. There are a few strong lads, who are willing and eager to go, and two fishermen; but there are only six in all, and they don't know if it is enough. Oh, dear! oh, dear! And those poor people in the ship! Must they all be drowned?"

"I think not," answered Monica, quietly.

"I think some means will be found to save them. Where is Randolph?"

Randolph was beside her next moment.

"Ah, if only I were a man," Beatrice was saying, excitedly. "Ah! why are women so useless, so helpless? To think of them drowning within sight of land— and they say the sea does not run so very high. Oh, what will they do? They cannot let them drown! Randolph, can nothing be done?"

"Yes, something can be done," he answered steadily and cheerfully. "The boat is being run down. It will not be difficult or dangerous to launch her in shelter of the cliff. There are six men to man it—all they want is a coxswain. Monica," he added, turning to her, and taking both her hands in his strong clasp, "you have

taught me to navigate the Bay of Trevlyn
so well, that I am equal to take that task
upon myself. There are lives to be saved
—the danger to the rescuing party is small,
they say so, and I believe they speak the
truth. Will you let me go ?"

She looked up to him with a mute entreaty in her eyes.

"There are lives to be saved, my
Monica," he said, with grave gentleness.
"Are our brothers to go down within
sight of land, without one effort on our
part to save them? Have you not wept
for such scenes before now? Have you no
pity to-night? Monica, in that vessel on
the rocks there are men, perhaps, whose
wives are waiting at home for them, and
praying for their safety. Will you let me
go ?"

She spoke at length with manifest effort, though her manner was quite calm.

"Is there no one else?"

"There is no one else."

For perhaps ten seconds there was perfect silence between them.

"Then Randolph, I will let you go."

He bent his head and kissed her.

"I knew my wife would bid me do my duty," he said proudly; "and believe me, my life, the danger is not great, and already the wind seems abating. It is but a small vessel. In all probability one journey will suffice. We shall not be out of sight, save for the darkness; we shall be under the lee of the cliff for the best part of the way. The boat is sound, the men know their work. We shall soon be back in safety, please God, and then you will be glad that you let me go."

She lifted her head and looked at him.

" Take me with you, Randolph.

" My darling, I cannot. It would not be right. We must not load the boat needlessly, even were there no other reason. Your presence there would take away half my courage, and perhaps it might necessitate leaving behind some poor fellow who otherwise might be saved."

Monica said no more. She knew that he spoke the truth.

Her white, still face with its stricken look, went to his heart. He knew how strangely nervous she was on wild, windy nights. He knew it would be hard for her to let him go, but she had shown herself his brave, true Monica, as he knew she

31*

would do, and now the kindest thing he could do was to shorten the parting, and return to her as quickly as his errand would allow him.

He held her a moment in his strong arms.

"Good-bye, my Monica, my own sweet wife. Keep up a brave heart. Kiss me once and let me go. Whatever happens, we are in God's hands. Remember that always."

She lifted her pale face, there was something strangely pathetic in its haunting beauty.

"Let me see you smile before I go. Tell me again that you bid me do my duty."

Suddenly the old serenity and peace came back to the upturned face. The smile he asked for shone in her sweet eyes.

"Good-bye, my Randolph—my husband
—good-bye. Yes, I do bid you do your
duty. May God bless and keep you
always."

For a moment they stood together, heart
pressed to heart, their lips meeting in one
long, lingering kiss; for one moment a
strange shadow as of farewell seemed to
hang upon them, and they clung together
as if no power on earth could separate
them.

The next moment he was gone, and
Monica, left alone, stretched out her hands
in the darkness.

"Oh, my love! my love!"

It was the one irrepressible cry from
the depths of her heart; the next moment
she repeated dreamily to herself the words
that had lately passed her husband's lips:

" ' Whatever happens, we are in God's hands. Remember that always.' Randolph, I will! I will! "

A ringing cheer told her that the boat was off. Nobody had seen the slim figure that had slunk after Randolph down to the beach. No one, in the darkness and general excitement, had seen that same slim figure leap lightly and noiselessly into the boat, and crouch down in the extreme end of the bow.

Conrad Fitzgerald had witnessed the parting between husband and wife; he had heard every word that had passed between them; and now, as he crouched with a tiger-like ferocity in the bottom of the boat, he muttered:

" This time he shall not escape me ! "

CHAPTER THE TWENTY-FIFTH.

THE boat launched by the rescuing party vanished in the darkness. Monica stood where her husband had left her in the shelter of the cliff, her pale face turned seawards, her eyes fixed upon the glimmering crests of the great waves, as they came rolling calmly in, in their resistless might and majesty.

Beatrice had twice come back to her, to assure her with eager vehemence that the danger was very slight, that it was lessening every moment as the wind shifted and abated in force—dangerous, indeed, for the poor fellows in the doomed vessel that had struck upon the fatal reef, but not very perilous for the willing and eager and experienced crew that had started off to rescue them. Beatrice urged this many times upon Monica; but the latter stood quite still and spoke not a word; only gazed out to sea with the same strange yearning gaze that was like a mute farewell.

Was it only an hour ago that she had been with her husband at home, telling him of the dim foreboding of coming woe that had haunted her all that day? It seemed to her as if she had all her life been standing beside the dark margin of this tempest-tossed sea, waiting the return of him who made all the happiness of her life—and waiting in vain.

Beatrice looked at her once or twice, but

did not speak again. Presently she moved down towards the water's edge. Surely the boat would be coming back now !

Suddenly there was a glad shout of triumph and joy from the fisher-folk, down by the brink of the sea.

"Here she is!" "Here she comes!" "Steady, there!" "Ease her a bit!" "This way now!" "Be ready, lads!" "Here she comes!" "Now, then, all together!" "After this wave—now!"

Cries, shouts, an eager confusion of tongues—the grating of a boat's keel upon the beach, and then a ringing hearty cheer.

"All safe?"

"All saved—five of them and a lad." "Just in time only." "She wouldn't have floated five minutes longer." "She was going down like lead."

What noise and confusion there was—
people crowding round, flitting figures
passing to and fro in the obscurity, every
one talking, all speaking together—such a
hubbub as Beatrice had never witnessed
before. She stood in glad, impatient
expectancy on the outskirts of the little
crowd. Why did not Randolph come away
from them to Monica? Why did she not
hear his voice with the rest? Her heart
gave a sudden throb as of terror.

"Where is Lord Trevlyn?"

Her voice, sharpened by the sudden fear
that had seized her, was heard through all
the eager clamour of those who stood round.
A gleam of moonlight, struggling through
the clouds, lighted up the group for a
moment. The words went round like wild-
fire: "Where is Lord Trevlyn?" and men

looked each other in the face, growing pale with conscious bewilderment. Where, indeed, was Lord Trevlyn? He was certainly not amongst them; yet he had undoubtedly steered the boat to shore. Where was he now? Men talked in loud, rapid tones. Women ran hither and thither, wringing their hands in distressful excitement, hunting for the missing man with futile eagerness. What had happened? Where could he be?

Suddenly a deep silence fell upon all; for in the brightening moonlight they saw that Monica stood amongst them—pale, calm and still, as a spirit from another world.

"Tell me," she said.

The story was told by one and another. Monica was used to the people and their ways. She gathered without difficulty the substance of the story. The boat had reached, without over-much difficulty or danger, the sinking vessel. She was a small coaling ship, with a crew of seven men and a boy. Two of the former had already been washed away, and the vessel was sinking rapidly. The five survivors were easily rescued; but the lad was entangled in the rigging, and was too much exhausted to free himself and follow. Lord Trevlyn was the first to realise this, and he sprang out of the boat at some peril to himself to the lad's assistance. Nobody had been able to see in the darkness what had passed, but all agreed that the lad had been handed to those in the boat by a pair of strong arms, and that after an interval of about three minutes— for the boat had swung round, and had to be brought back again, which took a little time—a man had sprung back into the boat, had shouted " All right ! " had seized the tiller, and sung out to the crew to " Give way, and put off ! " which they had done immediately, glad enough to be clear of the masts of the sinking vessel, which were in dangerous proximity.

No one had been able in the darkness to see the face of the steersman ; but all agreed that the voice was " a gentleman's " ; and most mysterious of all was the fact that the boat had been steered to shore with a skill that showed a thorough knowledge of the coast, and that not a man of those who now stood round had ever laid a hand upon the tiller.

A thrill of superstitious awe ran round as this fact became known, together with the terrible certainty that Lord Trevlyn had *not* returned with them. Was it indeed a phantom hand that had guided the frail bark through the wild, tossing waves? The bravest man there felt a shiver of awe—the women sobbed, and trembled unrestrainedly.

The boat was put to sea once more without a moment's delay. The wind was dropping, the tide had turned, and the danger was well nigh over. But heads were shaken in mute despair, and old men shook their heads at the bare idea of the survival of any swimmer, who had been left to battle with the waves round the sunken reef on a stormy winter's night.

Monica stood like a statue; she heeded neither the wailing of the women, the murmurs of sympathy from the men, nor the clasp of Beatrice's hand round her cold fingers. She saw nothing, heard nothing, save the tossing, the moaning of the pitiless sea.

The boat came back at last—came back in dead, mournful silence. That silence said all that was needed.

Monica stepped towards the weary, dejected men, who had just left the boat for the second time.

"You have done all that you could," she said gently. "I thank you from my heart."

And then she turned quietly away to go home—alone.

No one dared follow her too closely; even Beatrice kept some distance behind, sick with misery and sympathetic despair. Monica's step did not falter. She went back to the spot where her husband had left her, and stood still, looking out over the sea.

"Good-bye, my love—my own dear love," she said, very softly and calmly. "It has come at last, as I knew it would, when he held me in his arms for the last time on earth. Did he know it, too? I think he did just at the last. I saw it in his brave, tender face as he gave me that last kiss. But he died doing his duty. I will bear it for his sake." Yet with an irrepressible gesture of anguish she held out her arms in the darkness, crying out, not loud, indeed, but from the very depth of her broken heart, "Ah, Randolph!— husband—my love! my love!"

That was all; that one passionate cry of sorrow. After it calmness returned to her once more. She stepped towards Beatrice, who stood a little way off, and held out her hand.

"Come, dear," she said. "We must go home."

Beatrice was more agitated than Monica. She was convulsed with tearless sobs. She could only just command herself to stumble uncertainly up the steep cliff path that Monica trod with ease and freedom.

The moon was shining clearly now. She could see the gaze that her companion turned for one moment over the tossing waste of waters. She caught the softly-whispered words, "Good-bye, dear love! good bye!" and a sudden burst of tears came to her relief; but Monica's eyes were dry.

As they entered the castle hall, they saw

that the ill news had preceded them. Pale-
faced servants, both men and women,
stood awed and trembling, waiting, as
it seemed, for their mistress. A sound
as of hushed weeping greeted them as they
entered.

No one ever forgot the look upon
Monica's face as she entered her desolated
home. It was far more sad in its unutter-
able calm than the wildest expression of
grief could have been. Nobody dared to
speak a word, save the old nurse who had
tended Randolph from childhood. She
stepped forward, the tears streaming down
her wrinkled cheeks.

"Oh, my lady! my lady!" she sobbed.

Monica paused, looked for one moment
at the faithful servant; then bent her head,
and kissed her.

"Dear nurse," she said gently, "you always loved him;" and then she passed quietly on to the music-room—the room that she and her husband had quitted together less than three hours before, and shut herself up there—alone.

Beatrice dared not follow. She let Wilberforce take her upstairs, and tend her like a child, whilst they mingled their tears together over the brave young life cut short in its manhood's strength and prime. Randolph's nurse was no stranger to Beatrice, and it was easy for the good woman to speak with authority to one whom she had known as a child, force her to take some nourishment, and exchange wet garments for dry. She could not be induced to go to bed, exhausted though she was, but the wine and soup did her good,

32*

and the hearty burst of weeping had relieved her overcharged heart. She felt more like herself when, after an hour's time, she went downstairs again; but, oh! what a different house it was from what it had been a few hours back!

It was by that time eleven o'clock. Monica was still shut up in the music-room. Nothing had been heard of Haddon; she had hardly even given him a thought. She went down slowly to the hall, and found herself face to face with Tom Pendrill. He wore his hat and great coat. He had evidently just arrived in haste. As he removed the former she was startled at the look upon his face. She had not believed it capable of expressing so much feeling.

"Beatrice," he said hoarsely, "is it true?"

He did not know he had called her by her Christian name, and she hardly noticed it at the moment. She only bent her head and answered:

" Yes, it is true."

Together they passed into the lighted drawing-room, and stood on either side the glowing hearth, looking at each other fixedly.

" Where is Monica ? "

" In the music-room, alone. They were there together when the guns began. It will kill her, I am certain it will! "

" No," answered Tom quietly ; " she will not die. It would be happier for her if she could."

Beatrice looked at him with quivering lips.

" Oh ! " she said at last. " You understand her ? "

"Yes," he answered absently, looking away into the fire. "I understand her. She will not die."

Both were very silent for a time. Then he spoke.

"You were there?"

"Yes."

"Tell me about it."

"You have not heard?"

"Only the barest outline. Sit down and tell me all."

She did not resent his air of anthority. She sat down, and did his bidding. Tom listened in deep silence, weighing every word.

He made no comment on the strange story; but a very dark shadow rested upon his sharp featured face.

He was a man of keen observation and

acuteness of perception, and his mind often leaped to a conclusion that no present premises seemed to justify. Not for a moment would he have given utterance to the question that had suggested itself to his mind; but there it was, repeating itself again and again with persistent iteration.

" Can there have been foul play ? "

He spoke not a word, his face told no tales ; but he was musing intently. Where was that half mad fellow, Fitzgerald; who some months ago had seemed on the high-road to drink himself to madness or death? He had not been heard of for some time past; but Tom could not get the question out of his mind.

In the deep silence that reigned in the room every sound could be heard distinctly.

Beatrice suddenly started, for they were aware that the door of the music-room had been opened, and that Monica was coming towards them. The girl turned pale, and looked almost frightened. Tom stood up as his hostess appeared, setting his face like a flint.

The long hour that had seemed like a life-time to the wife—the widow—how could they bring themselves to think of her as such?—had left no outward traces upon Monica. Her face was calm and still, and very pale, but it was not convulsed by grief, and her eyes did not look as though they had shed tears, although there was no hardness in their depths. They shone with something of star-like brightness, at once soft and brilliant. The sweet serenity that had long been the habitual expression of her face seemed intensified rather than changed.

"Beatrice," she said quietly, "where is your brother?"

"I don't know."

"Has he not come in?"

"Not that I know of."

"We must inquire. He has been so many hours gone. I am uneasy about him."

"Oh, never mind about him," said Beatrice, quickly. "He will be all right."

"We must think of him," she answered. "Tom, it was good of you to come back. What brought you? Did you hear?"

"I heard a rumour. Of course I came back. Is there anything I can do?" He spoke abruptly, like a man labouring under some weight of oppression.

"I wish you would go and inquire for Lord Haddon. Randolph sent him to the life-boat station, because he believed he would ride over faster than anybody else. I think he should be followed now, if he has not come back. I cannot think what can have detained him so long."

"I will go and make inquiries," said Tom.

"Thank you. I should be much obliged if you would."

But as it turned out, there was no need for him to do this. Even as Monica spoke they became aware of a slight stir in the hall. Uncertain, rapid steps crossed the intervening space, and the next moment Haddon stood before them in the doorway, white, drenched, dishevelled, exhausted;

leaning as if for support against the framework, whilst his eyes sought those of his sister with a strange look of dazed horror.

"Beatrice!" he cried, in a strained, unnatural tone. "Say it is not true!"

Monica had stepped forward, anxious and startled at his appearance. The look upon her face must have brought conviction home to Haddon's heart, and this terrible conviction completed the work begun by previous over-fatigue and exhaustion. He made two uncertain steps forward, looked round him in a dazed bewildered way; then putting his hand to his head with a sudden gesture as of pain, called out :

" I say, what is it ?—Look out!" and Tom had only just time to spring forward and guide his fall as he dropped in a dead faint upon the couch hard by.

"Poor boy!" said Monica gently; "the shock has been too much for him."

CHAPTER THE TWENTY-SIXTH.

MONICA.

LORD HADDON was carried upstairs by Tom's direction, and put to bed at once, but it was a very long time before he recovered consciousness, and the doctor's face was grave when he rejoined Monica and Beatrice an hour later.

Afterwards they learned that he had reached the life-boat station, only to find the boat out in another direction, that he had lost his way in the darkness, and had been riding for hours over trackless moors, wet through by driving storms of rain, obliged often to halt, despite the cold and

wet, to wait for passing gleams of moonlight to show him his way; and this after
a long day's shooting and a long fast. He
had reached the castle at last, utterly worn
out and exhausted, only to hear the terrible
news of the death of his best friend. The
strain had been too much, and he had
given way.

He awoke to consciousness only in a
high state of fever, with pain in every
joint; and Beatrice, in answer to Tom's
question, admitted that her brother had
had a sharp attack of rheumatic fever some
three years before, and had always been
rather susceptible to cold and damp ever
since.

Tom looked gravely at Monica.

"I was afraid he was in for something of
that kind."

"Poor boy!" she said again, very gently. "I am so sorry. You will stay with us, Tom? It will be a comfort to have you."

"Of course I will stay," he answered, in his abruptest fashion. "I shall sit up with Haddon to night. You two must go to bed at once—I insist upon it."

"Come, Beatrice," said Monica, holding out her hand. "We must obey orders you see."

As they went together up the broad staircase, Beatrice said, with a little sob:

"I cannot bear to think of our giving you all this trouble—just now."

But Monica stopped her by a kiss.

"Have you not learned by this time Beatrice, that the greatest help in bearing our own sorrows is to help others with their burdens? I am grieved for you, dear, that this other trouble should have come ; but Tom is very clever, and we will all nurse him back to health again. Good-night, dearest. You must try to sleep, that you may be strong to-morrow."

The next day Lord Haddon was very ill —dangerously ill—the fever ran very high, other unfavourable symptoms had showed themselves. Tom's face was grave and absorbed, and Raymond, who came over at his brother's request, looked even more anxious. Yet possibly this alarming illness of a guest beneath her roof was the very best thing that could have happened, as far at Monica herself was concerned. But for his illness, Beatrice and her brother must have left Trevlyn at once ; it was probable that Monica would have elected to remain there entirely alone during the early days of her widowhood, alone in her own desolation, more heart-breaking to witness than any wild abandonment of grief, alone without even those last melancholy offices to perform, without even the solemn pageantry of a funeral to give some little occupation to the mind, or to bring home in its own incontrovertible way the fact that a loved being has passed away from the world for ever.

Randolph had, as it were, vanished from this life almost as if spirited away. There was nothing to be done, no obsequies to be performed. For just a few days a faint glimmer of hope existed in some minds that a passing vessel might have picked him up, that a telegram announcing his safety might yet arrive ; but at the end of a week every spark of such hope had died out, and Monica, who had never from the first allowed herself to be so buoyed up, put on her heavy widow's weeds with the steady unflinching calmness that had characterised her throughout.

She devoted herself to the task of nursing Lord Haddon, in which task she showed untiring care and skill. All agreed that it was best for her to have her thoughts and attention occupied in some quiet labour of love like this, and certainly her skill at this time was such as to render her services almost invaluable to the patient.

Haddon lay for weeks in a very critical state, racked with pain and burning with fever. Without being always delirious, he was not in any way master of himself, and no one could soothe, or quiet, or compose him, during these long, weary days, except Monica. She seemed to possess a power that acted upon him like a charm. He might not always know her—very often he did not appear to recognise her, but he always felt her influence. At her bidding he would cease the restless tossing and muttering that exhausted his strength and gave him much needless pain. He would take from her hand food that no one else could persuade him to touch. She could often soothe him to sleep, simply by the sound of her voice, or the touch of her hand upon his burning brow.

"If he pulls through it will be your doing," Tom sometimes said to her. And Monica felt she could not do enough for the youth, who had suffered all this in carrying out her husband's last command, and who

33*

had succumbed when his task was done, in hearing of the fate that had befallen his friend

A curious bond seemed established be-tween those two, the power of which he felt with a throb of keen joy almost akin to pain, when at last the fever was subdued, and he began to know in a feeble, uncertain sort of fashion, what it was that had happened, and how life had been going with him during the past weeks.

It was of Monica he asked the account of that terrible night, and from her lips he learned the story to which none else had dared to allude in her presence. It was he who talked to her of Randolph, recalled incidents of the past, talked of their boyish days and the escapades they had indulged together, passing on to the increase of mutual understanding and affection that had bound them together as manhood advanced.

Nobody else talked to her like this. Haddon never could have done so, had not weakness and illness brought them into such close communion one with another. His feelings towards Monica were those of simple adoration — he worshipped the very ground she trod on. He often felt that to die with her hand upon his head, her eyes looking gently and kindly into his, was all and more than he could wish. His intense loving devotion gave him a sort of insight into her true nature, and he knew by instinct that he did not hurt her when he talked to her of him who was gone. Perhaps from no other lips could Monica have borne that name to be spoken just then; but Haddon in his hours of wandering had talked so much of Randolph, that she had grown used to hear him speak of the husband she had loved and lost, and she knew by the way in which he had betrayed himself then how deeply and truly he loved him.

When the fever had gone, and the patient lay white and weak, hardly able to move or speak, yet with a mind cleared from the haunting shadows of delirium, eager to know the history of all that had passed, it had not seemed very hard then, in answer to the wistful look in the big grey eyes, and the whispered words from the pale lips to tell him all the truth; and the ice once broken thus, it had been no effort to talk of Randolph afterwards, and to let Haddon talk of him too.

This outlet did her good. She was

not a woman to whom talking was a necessity, yet it was better for her to speak sometimes of the sorrow that was weighing upon her crushed spirit; and it was far, far easier to do this to a listener like Haddon, who from his weakness and prostration could rise to no great heights of sympathy, could offer no attempt at consolation, could only look at her with wistful earnestness, and murmur a broken word from time to time, than it would have been to those who would have met her with a burst of tears, or with those quiet caresses and marks of sympathy that must surely have broken down her hardly-won composure and calm.

So this illness of Haddon's had really been a boon to her, and perhaps to others as well; but for a few weeks Monica's life seemed passed in a sort of dream, and she was able to notice but little that passed around her. She was wrapped in a strange trance—she lived in the past with her husband, who sometimes hardly seemed to have left her. Only when ministering to the needs of the young earl did she arouse herself from her waking dream, and even then it sometimes seemed as if the dream were the reality, and the reality a dream.

Tom was a great deal at Trevlyn just now. For a long time Haddon's condition was so exceedingly critical that his presence was almost a necessity, and when the patient gradually became convalescent, Monica needed his help in getting through the business formalities that began to crowd upon her when all hopes of Randolph's rescue became a thing of the past.

Monica was happy at least in this—there

was no need for her to leave her old home
—no new earl to claim Trevlyn, and banish
her from the place she loved best in the
world. The Trevlyns were a dying race,
as it seemed. Randolph and Monica were
the last of their name, and the entail
expired with him. Trevlyn was hers, as
well as all her husband's property. She
was a rich woman, but in the first instance
it was difficult to understand the position,
and she naturally turned in her perplexity
to Tom Pendrill, who was a thorough man
of business, shrewd and hard-headed, and
who, from his long acquaintance and connection with Trevlyn, understood more
about the estate than anybody else she
could have selected. He was very good to
her, as she always said. He put himself
entirely at her disposal, and played the

part of a kind and wise brother. His dry, matter-of-fact manner of dealing with transfer of property, and such-like matters, was in itself a comfort. She was never afraid of talking things over with him. He kept sentiment studiously and entirely in the back-ground. Although she knew perfectly that his sympathy for her was very great, he never obtruded it upon her in the least; it was offered and accepted in perfect silence on both sides.

Mrs. Pendrill, too, was a good deal at Trevlyn. She yearned over Monica in the days of her early widowhood, and she had grown very fond of Beatrice and her brother. Haddon wanted so very much care and nursing that Mrs. Pendrill's presence in the house was often a help to all. Whilst Monica was in the sick room, she and

Beatrice spent many long hours together, and strange intimacy of thought sprang up between those two who were so far fromeach other in age and position. Haddon, too, was fond of the gentle-faced old lady, and he loved sometimes to get her all to herself, and make her talk to him of Monica.

His illness had left its traces upon the earl. He had, despite his five-and-twenty years, seemed but a lad all this while ; but when he left his bed, it was curious to see how much of boyishness had passed out of his face, how much quiet, thoughtful manliness had taken its place.

Nobody quite knew how or why this change had been so marked. Perhaps the shock of his friend's death had had something to do with it : perhaps the danger he had himself been in. Very near indeed to the gates of death had the young man stood. He had almost trodden the shadowy valley, even though his steps had been retraced to the land of the living. Perhaps it was this knowledge that made him pass as it were in one bound from boyhood to manhood—or was there some other cause at work?

His face wore a look of curious purpose and resolution, oddly combined with a sort of mute, determined patience: his pale, sharpened face, that had changed so much during the past weeks, was changed in expression even more than in contour. His grey eyes, once always full of boyish merriment and laughter, were grave and earnest now: the eyes of a man full of thought, expressive of a hidden yet resolute

purpose. These hollow eyes followed Monica
about with unconscious persistency, and
rested upon her with a sense of perfect
content. When he grew a little stronger,
and could just rise from the sofa and trail
himself across the room, it was strange to
mark how eager he was to render her
those little instinctive attentions that come
naturally from a man to a woman.

Sometimes Monica would accept them
with a smile, oftener she would restrain
him with a gentle commanding gesture, and
bid him keep quiet till he was stronger;
but she accepted his chivalrous admiration
in the spirit in which it was offered, and
let him look upon himself as her especial
knight, as well he might, since to her skill
and care Tom plainly told him he owed his
life.

She let him talk to her of Randolph, though none of the others dared to breathe that name. Sometimes she played to him in the dimness of the music-room—and even he hardly knew how privileged he was to be admitted there. She regarded him in the light of a loved brother, and felt tenderly towards him, as one who had done and suffered much in the same cause that had cost her gallant husband his life. What he felt towards her would be more difficult to analyse. At present he simply worshipped her, with a humble, devout singleness of purpose that elevated his whole nature. The vague, fleeting, distant hope that some day it might be given to him to comfort her had hardly yet entered into the region of conscious thought.

CHAPTER THE TWENTY-SEVENTH

HAUNTED.

CHRISTMAS had come and gone whilst Lord Haddon lay hovering between life and death. As the year turned, he began to regain health and strength; but his progress was exceedingly slow, and all idea of leaving Trevlyn was for the present entirely out of the question. A journey in mid-winter was not to be thought of. It would be enough to bring the whole illness back again; and Monica would not listen when he sometimes said, with diffidence and appeal, that he feared they were encroaching too much upon her hospitality and goodness. In truth, neither brother nor sister were in haste to leave Trevlyn, or to leave Monica alone in her desolate widowhood; and as Haddon's state of health rendered a move out of the question, the situation was accepted with the more readiness.

Monica was able now to resume something of the even tenor of her way, to take up her daily round of duties, and shape out her life in accordance with her strangely altered circumstances.

All the old sense of dread connected with the sea had now vanished entirely. It never frowned upon her now. It was her friend always—the haunting presentiment of dread had passed away with the actual certainty. Henceforward nothing could hold for her any great measure of terror.

She had passed through the very worst already.

Sometimes Monica had a strange feeling that she was not alone during her favourite twilight pacings by the sea. She had a sense of being watched — followed — and the uneasiness of the dogs added to this impression. It troubled her but little, however. She had no fears for herself—she knew, too, that she was a little fanciful, and that it was hardly likely in reality that her footsteps were dogged.

But one dim January evening, as she pursued her way along the margin of the sea, she was startled by seeing some large object lying dark upon the pebbly beach. Her heart beat more fast than was its wont, for she saw as she approached that it was

the figure of a man, lying face downwards
upon the damp stones.

He did not look like a fisherman, he was
too well dressed, and there seemed something not altogether unfamiliar in the
aspect of the slight, well-proportioned
figure. For a moment she could not recall
the association, but as the dogs ran up
snuffing and growling, the man started and
sat up, revealing the pale, haggard face of
Conrad Fitzgerald.

Monica recoiled with an instinctive
gesture of aversion. She had not seen
him since those summer days when she had
been haunted by the vision of his vindictive
face and sinister eyes. But how he had
changed since then! She could not help
looking at him, he was so pale, so thin;
his face was lined as if by pain, and his

fiery eyes were set in deep hollows. There was something rather awful in his appearance, yet he did not look so wicked, so repulsive, as he had done many times before.

A strange look of terror gleamed in his eyes as they met those of Monica.

"Go away!" he cried wildly. "What do you come here for? Why do you look at me like that? Go—in mercy, go!"

Monica was startled at his wild words and looks. Surely he was mad. But if so, she must show no fear of him; she knew enough to be aware of that.

"What are you doing out here in the dark?" she said. "You ought not to be lying there this cold night. You had better go home, or you will lose your way in the dark."

34*

He laughed wildly.

" Lose my way in the dark! It is always dark now—always, since that dark night —ha! ha!—that night!" His laugh was terrible in its wild despair. " Why do you look at me? Why do you speak to me? You should not! You should not! You would not if——oh, God! are you a ghost too?"

Such an awful look of horror shone out of his eyes that Monica's blood ran cold. His gaze was fixed on vacancy. He looked straight at her, yet as if he did not see her, but something beyond. The anguish and despair painted upon that wild, yet still beautiful, face smote Monica's heart with a sense of deep sorrow and pity.

" I am no ghost, Conrad," she answered gently, trying if the sound of the old name would drive that wild madness out of his eyes. "Why are you afraid? What are you looking at? There is nothing there."

For his eyes were still glaring wildly into the darkness beyond, and as Monica spoke he lifted his arm, and pointed to something out at sea.

"Don't look at me!" he whispered hoarsely, yet not as if he addressed Monica. "Don't speak to me! If you speak, I shall go mad! I shall go mad, I say! Why do you haunt me so? Why do you look always like that? I had a right—all is fair in love and war—and hate! Why did you give me the chance? I had a vow —a vow in heaven—or hell! Ah! ha! Revenge is sweet, after all!" and he burst into a wild, discordant laugh, dreadful to hear.

Monica shuddered, a sense of horror creeping over her. She did not catch the whole of his words, lost as that hoarse whisper was sometimes in the sullen plash of the advancing waves. The words were not addressed to her, but to some imaginary object visible only to the eye of madness. She attached no meaning to what she heard. She had no clue by which to unravel the workings of his disordered mind. Yet it was terrible to see his terror-stricken face, and listen to the exclamations addressed to a phantom foe. She tried to recall him to himself.

" Conrad, there is no one here but ourselves. You have been dreaming."

Conrad turned his wild eyes towards her, but continued to point wildly over the sea.

"Can you not see him? There—out there! His head—his eyes—ah, those eyes!—as he looked *then*—then! Ah, don't look so at me, I say! You will kill me!"

He buried his face in his hands and shuddered from head to foot. Monica, despite the shiver of horror that crept over her, felt more strongly than anything else a deep pity for one whose mind was so visibly shattered. Much of the past could be condoned to one whose mental faculties were so terribly unstrung. She came one step nearer, and laid her hand upon his arm.

"You should not be out here alone," she said. "You had better go home. It is growing dark already. If you will come with me to the lodge, I will see that you

have a lantern ; or, if you like, I will send
a servant with a lantern with you." She
felt, indeed, that he was hardly in a condition to be out alone. She wished Tom
Pendrill could see him now. But at the
touch of her hand Conrad sprang back as
if she had struck him. His eyes were
full of shrinking horror.

"Go away !" he said fiercely, "your
hand burns me—it burns me, I say ! How
can you look at me or touch me ? What
have I done that you come here day by
day to torment me ? Is it not enough that
he leaves me no peace night or day ?—that
he brings me down to this cursed place,
whether I will or no, but you must haunt
me too ? Ah, it is too much—it is too
much, I say !"

She could not catch all these rapidly-uttered words, but she read the hopeless misery of his face.

" I do not wish to distress you, Conrad. Will you go home quietly now ? You are not well ; you should not be out here alone. Have you anybody there to take care of you ? "

He laughed again, and flung his arms above his head with a wild gesture of despair.

" You say this to me—you ! you ! It only wanted this. My God, this is too much ! "

He turned from her and sprang away in the darkness. She heard his steps as he dashed recklessly up the cliff path—so recklessly that she half expected to hear the sound of a slip and a fall—and then as he reached the summit and turned inland, they died away into silence.

Monica drew a long breath of relief when she found herself alone. There was something expressibly awful in talking alone to a madman in the dimness of the dying day, in hearing his wild words addressed to some phantom shadow seen only by his disordered vision. She shivered a little as she turned towards him. She could stay no longer in that lonely place.

She met Tom looking out for her on her return. He said something about her staying out too long in the darkness. She laid her hand upon his arm, and pacing up and down the dark avenue, she told him of her adventure with the madman.

"Tom, I am certain he ought to see a doctor. Will you not see if you can do something for him?"

She could not see the expression of Tom's

face. Had she been able to do so, she would have been startled. His voice was very cold as he answered :

" I am not a lunacy commissioner, Monica."

She was surprised, and a little hurt.

" You are very hard, Tom. You saw him once before, why not again ? "

" If he, or his friends for him, require medical advice, I suppose they are capable of sending for it," he said, adding with sudden fierceness, as it seemed to her, " Monica, Conrad Fitzgerald, ill or well, is nothing to you. It is not fit you should waste a single thought upon that scoundrel again ! "

She was surprised at his vehemence ; it was so unlike Tom to speak with heat. What had there been in her account of

the meeting to discompose him so greatly?
Before she could attempt to frame the
question, he had asked one of her—asked
it abruptly, as it seemed irrelevantly.

" How long has Fitzgerald been in these
parts ? "

" I don't know ?   I have never seen him
till to-night, nor heard of him at all ? "

" Nor I.   Go in, Monica.   It is too late
for you to be out."

" And you ? "

" I will come presently."

" And you will think about what I asked
you ? "

" I will think about it—yes."

The tone was enigmatic.   She could not
make Tom out at all, but she went in at
his bidding.   She knew that he wished to
be alone, that he had something disturb-

ing upon his mind, though what it was she could not divine.

Tom, as it turned out, had no choice in the matter; for his brother sent to him next day a message to the effect that Fitzgerald's servant had been to him with a very sad account of his master, who seemed to be suffering under an acute attack of delirium tremens. Raymond thought his brother, who had seen him once before, had better go the next day in a casual sort of way, and see if he could do anything. Fitzgerald was furious at the idea of having a doctor near him; but possibly he would not regard Tom in that light, and the servants would do all they could to obtain for him access to their master. They were terrified at his ravings, and half afraid he would do himself or them an injury if not placed under proper control.

So Tom, upon the following afternoon, started for the old dilapidated house, without saying a word to anyone as to his destination, and was eagerly admitted by a haggard-looking servant, who said that his master was " terrible bad to-day—it was awful like to hear him go on," and expressed it as his opinion that he was almost past knowing who was near him, he was so wild and delirious. He had kept his bed for the past two days, having been very ill since coming in, wet and exhausted, on the night Monica had seen him. Between the attacks of delirium he was as weak as a child ; and with this much of warning and explanation, Tom was ushered upstairs.

An hour later he left that desolate

house with a quick, firm tread, that broke,
as he turned a corner and was concealed
from view, almost to a run. His face was
very pale; it looked thinner and sharper
than it had done an hour before, and his
eyes were full of an unspeakable horror.
Now and again a sort of shudder ran
through his frame; but no word passed
his tightly-compressed lips. He hurried
through the tangled park as if some
deadly malaria lurked there. He hardly
drew his breath until he had left the
trees and brake behind, and had
plunged into the wild trackless moor;
even then, goaded by his thoughts, he
plunged blindly along for a mile or more,
until at last, breathless and exhausted, he
sank face downwards upon the heather,
trembling in every limb.

How long he lay there he never knew. He was roused at last by a touch upon his shoulder, and raising himself with a start, he looked straight into the startled eyes of Beatrice Wentworth.

CHAPTER THE TWENTY-EIGHTH.

LOVERS.

Tom sprang to his feet, and the two stood gazing at one another for a moment in mute surprise.

" You are ill," said Beatrice ; " you are as white as a sheet. What is the matter ? "

She spoke anxiously. She looked half frightened at his strange looks ; he saw it, and recovered himself instantly. It was perhaps the first time he had ever been taken unawares, and he was not altogether pleased that it had happened now.

"What are you doing out here all alone?" he asked peremptorily.

"What are you doing lying on the ground on a cold January evening?" she retorted. "Do you want to get rheumatic fever, too?"

"Answer my question first. What are you doing out here, miles away from home, with the darkness coming on, too?"

"I lost my way," she answered carelessly. "I never can keep my bearings in these strange, wild places, where everything looks alike."

"Then I must take you home," said Tom shortly.

"You said you were going to dine at St. Maws to-night," she objected.

"I shall take you home first," he said.

"It will be ever so much out of your road. Just show me the way. I shall find it fast enough."

"I dare say—After having lost it in broad daylight. You must come with me. I cannot trust you."

Beatrice flushed hotly as she turned and walked beside him. Was more meant than met the ear?

"There is not the least need you should," she said haughtily, and seemed disposed to say no more.

Tom spoke first, spoke in his abrupt peremptory fashion. He was absorbed and distrait. She tried not to feel disappointed at his words.

"Lady Beatrice, is it true that you knew Randolph Trevlyn intimately for many years?"

35*

"Ever since I can remember. He was almost like a brother to us."

"Do you know if he ever had an enemy?"

Beatrice looked up quickly into his pale face.

"Why do you ask?"

"That is my affair. I do not ask without a reason. Think before you answer—if you can."

"Randolph was always such a favourite," she began, but was interrupted by a qnick impatient gesture from Tom.

"Don't chatter," he said, almost rudely, "think!"

Oddly enough this brusque reminder did not offend her. She saw that Tom's nerves were all on edge, that they were strung to a painful pitch of tension. She began to

catch some of his earnestness and deter-
mination.

Beatrice was taken out of herself, and
from that moment her manner changed for
the better. She thought the matter over
in silence.

"I have heard that Sir Conrad Fitzgerald had an old grudge against him.

" Ah ! " breathed Tom softly.

" But I fancied, perhaps, that Monica's
influence had made them friends. Randolph knew some disreputable story
connected with Sir Conrad's past life—
Haddon knows more about it than I do—
and he always hated him for it."

" Ah ! " said Tom again.

"Why do you ask ?" questioned Beatrice again ; but he gave her no answer.
He was wrapped in deep thought. She

looked at him once or twice, but said no
more. He was the first to speak, and the
question was a little significant.

"You were down on the shore with
Monica and Trevlyn that night, were you
not?"

"Yes."

"Was Fitzgerald there, too?"

She looked at him with startled eyes.

"No; certainly not."

"Can you be sure of that? Was there
moon enough to show plainly everything
that went on?"

Beatrice put up her hand to her head.

"No," she answered. "I ought not to
have spoken so positively. It was too
dark to see anything. There might have
been dozens of people there whom I might
never have seen. I was much too anxious

and excited to keep a sharp look-out—
why should I?—and there was not a gleam
of moonlight till many minutes after the
boat got back, and the confusion was very
great all the time. Why do you talk so ?
Why do you ask such a question?"

She spoke with subdued excitement and
insistance.

" *Somebody* was in that boat unknown
to the crew," he answered significantly.

" Was there ? "

" Somebody steered the boat to shore.
You do not share, I presume, in the
popular belief of the phantom coxswain?"

Beatrice stopped short, trembling and
scared.

" You think——? " but she could only
get out those two words ; she knew not how
to frame the question.

He bent his head. "I do."

But she put out her hand with a quick, passionate gesture, as if fighting with some hideous phantom.

"Ah! no! no! It could not be. It would be too unspeakably awful — too horrible! How do you know? How can you say such things? What has put such a hideous thought into your mind?"

"I came from standing by Fitzgerald's bed, listening to his words of wandering, his delirious outbursts. It is plain enough what phantoms are haunting him now—what pictures he is seeing, as he lies in the stupor of drink and opium. He is trying to drown thought and remorse, but he has not succeeded yet."

Beatrice shuddered strongly, and faltered

a little in her walk. Tom took her hand
and placed it within his arm.

" You are tired, Beatrice?"

"No; but it is so awful. Tom "—
calling him so as unconsciously as he had
called her Beatrice—" must Monica know
this? Oh! it was cruel enough before—
but this——"

"She shall never know," said Tom
quickly. " To what end should we add this
burden to what she carries now? No one
could prove it—it may be nothing more
than some sick fancy, engendered by the
thought of what might have been. Mind
you, I have no moral doubts myself; but
the man is practically mad, and no confession or evidence given by him would be
accepted. He has fulfilled his vow—he
has murdered—practically murdered his

foe ; but Monica must be spared the knowledge : she must never know."

" No, never! never!" cried Beatrice;
and her voice expressed so much feeling,
that Tom turned and looked at her in the
fading light.

" Have you a heart after all, Beatrice ? "
he asked.

She made no answer; her heart beat
wildly, answering in its own fashion the
question asked, but not in a way that he
could hear.

" Beatrice," rather fiercely, "why did
you not marry the marquis ? "

" Because I loathed him."

" You did not always loathe him ? "

" I did, I did, always."

" You flirted with him disgracefully,
then."

She looked up with something of pleading in her dark eyes.

" I was but eighteen."

" Do you never flirt now ? "

She looked up again, her eyes flashing strangely.

" What right have you to ask such a question? "

" The right of the man who loves you," he answered, in the same half-fierce, half-bitter way—" who loves you with every fibre of his being; and although he has proved you vain and frivolous and heartless once and again, cannot tear your image from his heart. Do not think I am complaining. I suppose you have a right to please yourself; but sometimes I feel as if no man had ever been treated so abominably as I have been by you."

" You by me ! " she answered, panting in her excitement, " when it was you who left me in a fury, without one word of farewell."

"I thought I had had my *congé* pretty distinctly."

" You had had nothing of the kind— nothing but a few wild confused words from a mere child, frightened and bewildered by happiness and nervousness into the silliest of speeches a silly girl could make at such a moment. But you cannot understand—you never will—you are made of stone, I think."

He turned upon her quickly.

" I wish I were, sometimes," he said ; "I wish it when I am near you. You make me love you—I am powerless in your hands, and you—you——"

" I love you with all my heart. I have never loved anybody else, and you have behaved cruelly, ·disgracefully to me always." The words came all at once in one vehement burst of passion.

He stopped short, wheeled round, and stood facing her. He could only just see her face as they stood thus in the gathering dusk.

" Beatrice," he said, slowly, ·" what did you say just now? Say it again."

Defiance shone out of her eyes.

" I will not !" she said, her cheeks flaming.

He took both her hands in his and held them hard.

" Yes you will," he answered. " Say it again."

She was panting with a strange mix-

ture of feeling; the earth and sky seemed
to spin round together.

"Say it again, Beatrice."

"I said—I loved you; but I don't—I
will never, never say it again——"

She got no farther, for he held her so
closely in his arms that all speech was impossible for the moment.

"That will do," he answered. "I
don't want you to say it again. Once is
enough."

*   *   *   *   *

"Monica," said Beatrice in the softest
of whispers as she came into the quiet
room where her brother lay asleep upon
the sofa, and Monica sat dreaming beside
the fire. "Ah, Monica, Monica!" and
then she stopped short, kneeling down,
and turning her quivering face and swim-

ming eyes towards the face bent tenderly over her.

Somehow it was never needful to say much to Monica. She always understood without many words. She bent her head now, and kissed Beatrice.

" Is it so, then, dear ? " she asked.

" Did you know ? "

" 1 knew what you told me yourself, and I could see for myself that he had not forgotten any more than you."

" I did not see it."

" Possibly not—neither did he ; but sometimes love is very blind—and very wilful too."

Was there a touch of tender reproach in the tone ? Beatrice looked at her earnestly.

" I know what you mean," she said.

"We both want to be master ; but I think—I am afraid—he will have the upper hand now."

But the smile that quivered over the upturned face was full of such sweetness and brightness that Monica kissed her again.

" You will not find him such a tyrant as he professes to be. Tom is very generous and unselfish, despite his affectation of cynicism. I am so glad you have made him happy at last. I am so glad that our paths in life will not lie very widely apart."

Beatrice took Monica's hand and kissed it.

"I am so happy," she said simply. " And I owe it all to you."

Monica caressed the dark head laid

against her knee, as Beatrice subsided into her favourite lowly position at Monica's feet. Presently she became aware that the girl's tears were falling fast.

" Crying, dearest ? " she questioned gently.

A stifled sob was the answer.

" What is the matter, my child?"

" Randolph! " was all that Beatrice could get out. Somehow the desolation of Monica's life had never come home to her with quite the same sense of realisation as now, in the hour of her deepest happiness.

" He would be glad," answered Monica, steadily and sweetly. " He loved you dearly, Beatrice ; and he and Tom were always such friends. It was his hope that all would come right. If he can see us now, as I often think he can, he will be rejoicing in your happiness now. You must shed no tears to-night, dearest, unless they are tears of happiness.

Beatrice suddenly half rose, and flung her arms round Monica.

"How can you bear it? How can you bear it? Monica, I think you are an angel. No one in this wide world was ever like you. And to think——" she shuddered strongly and stopped short.

"You are excited and over-wrought." said Monica gently. "You must not let yourself be knocked up, or Tom will scold me when he comes back. See, Haddon is waking up. He had such a bad headache, poor boy; I hope he has slept it off. You must tell him the news—it will please him I am sure."

"You tell him," whispered Beatrice, and slipped away to relieve her over-burdened heart by a burst of tears ; for one strange revelation following upon another had tried her more than she had known at the time.

Haddon was quietly pleased at the news. He liked Tom ; he had fancied that he and Beatrice were not altogether indifferent to each other, so this conclusion did not take him altogether by surprise. He was sorry to think of losing Beatrice, but not as perplexed as he would have been some months before. Life looked different to him now—more serious and earnest. He began to have aspirations of his own. He no longer regarded existence as a sort of pleasant easy game of play.

Certainly it seemed as if the course of

true love as regarded Beatrice and Tom, after passing its early shoals and quick-sands, were to run quietly and smoothly enough now. He came back from St. Maws in time for dinner, and when dessert was put on the table, he announced his plans with the hardihood characteristic of the man.

"Aunt Elizabeth is delighted, Beatrice, and so is Raymond," he said. "I have told them that we will be married almost at once, within two months, at least—oh, you needn't look like that. I think I've waited long enough—pretty well as long as Jacob——"

"Did for Leah—and didn't like her in the end—don't make that your precedent."

"Well, don't interrupt," proceeded Tom imperturbably. "We've got it all beautifully arranged. I'm going to take part of the regular practice, as Raymond has always been bothering me to do ever since it increased so much, and we're to have half the house for our establishment, and he and Aunt Elizabeth the other. It was originally two houses, and lends itself excellently to that arrangement, though I dare say practically we shall be all one household, as you and our aunt have managed to hit it off so well. Monica, can't Beatrice be married from Trevlyn when Haddon is well enough to give her away? It would save a lot of bother. I hate flummery, and I'm sure she does too. Come now, Beatrice, don't laugh. Don't you think that would be an excellent arrangement? Here we are ; what is the good of getting all split up again? You'll be losing your heart to

another marquis if I let you out of my
sight."

Her eyes were dancing with mischievous
merriment. She was more than ready to
enter the lists.

"Just listen to the tyrant—trying to
keep me a prisoner already! trying to take
everything into his own hands—and not
content without adding insult to injury!"

His eyes too were alight; but his mouth
was grim.

"I have not forgotten how you served
me last time, my lady."

"At Oxford?"

"At Oxford."

"Monica, listen. I will tell you how I
served him. I had eyes for no one but
him, silly girl that I was; I was with him
morning, noon and night. Child as I was

at the time, careless and inexperienced, even _I_ was absolutely ashamed at the open preference I showed him ; I blush even now to think of the undisguised way in which I flung myself at a particularly hard head. And yet he pretends he did not understand! If that is so, then for real, downright, hopeless stupidity and obtuseness, commend me to an Oxford double-first-class-man ! "

Beatrice might get the best of it in an encounter of tongues, but Tom had his own way in the settlement of their affairs, possibly because her resistance was but a pretence. What, indeed, had they to wait for, when they had been waiting so many long years for one another ? "

Nothing clouded the horizon of their happiness. Even the hideous shadow which

had been in a sense the means of bringing
them together seemed to have vanished
with the sudden disappearance of Conrad
Fitzgerald from the neighbourhood.   Upon
the very day following Tom's visit to him,
he left his house, ill and weak as he was,
to join his sister at Mentone.   His servant
accompanied him.   The desolate house
was shut up once more, and Tom Pendrill
sincerely hoped that the haunting baleful
influence of that wild and wicked nature
had passed from their lives for ever.

And Beatrice after all was married at
Trevlyn, in the little cliff church that had
seen the hands of Randolph and Monica
joined in wedlock.   She resisted a good
while, feeling afraid that it would be
painful to Monica—a second wedding, and
that within a few months of her own

widowhood. But Monica took part with
Tom, and the bride elect gave way,
only too delighted at heart to be with
Monica to the very last.

It was a very quiet wedding—as quiet
as Monica's own—even the people gathered
together in the little church had hardly
changed. Only one short year had passed
since Monica in her snowy robes had stood
before that little altar, with the marriage
vow upon her lips—only a year ago, and
now?

Yet Monica's face was very calm and
sweet. She shed no tears, she seemed to
have no sad thoughts for herself, however
others might feel. One pair of grey eyes
seldom wandered from her face as the simple
ceremonies of the day proceeded. One
heart was far more occupied with thoughts

of the pale-faced widow than of the bloom-
ing bride.

Haddon quitted Trevlyn almost immediately after his sister. The words of
thanks he tried to speak faltered on his
tongue, and would not come.

Monica understood, and answered by
one of her sweetest smiles.

"You were Randolph's friend; you are
my friend now. You must not try to
thank me. I am so very glad to think of
the link that binds us together. I shall
not lose sight of you whilst Beatrice is
so near. You will come again some
day?"

"Yes, Lady Trevlyn," he answered
quietly, "I will come again;" and he
raised the hand he held for one moment
very reverently to his lips.

As he drove away he looked back, and saw Monica still standing upon the terrace.

"Yes," he said quietly to himself, "I will come back—some day."

CHAPTER THE TWENTY-NINTH.

" AS WE FORGIVE."

A YEAR had passed away since that fatal
night when Randolph had left his wife
standing on the shore—had gone away in
the darkness and had returned no more :
a year had passed, with its chequered lights
and shades, but the anniversary of her
husband's death found Monica, as he had
left her, at Trevlyn—alone.

Many things had happened during that
year. Beatrice had married and settled
happily in the picturesque red house at
St. Maws as Tom Pendrill's loving, brilliant
wife. Monica had been to Germany once

again, to assure herself with her own eyes
of the truth of the favourable reports sent to
her. She had had the satisfaction of seeing
how great an improvement had taken
place in Arthur's condition ; that although
the cure was slow—would most likely need
a second, possibly even a third year before
it would be absolutely complete, yet it was
practically certain, if he and those who
held his fate in their hands would but
have patience and perseverance. The boy
was quite happy in the establishment of
which he was a member. He had gone
through the most trying part of the
treatment, and was enthusiastic about the
kindness and skill of his doctor. He had
made many friends, and had quite lost
the home-sickness that had occasionally
troubled him at first. He was delighted

to see Monica again.   He was insistant that
she should come to see him often; but he
did not even wish to return to Trevlyn till
he could do so whole and sound, as a man
in good health and strength, instead of a
helpless invalid.

Monica was summoned from Germany
by the news of the dangerous illness of
Lady Diana, who died only a few days
after the arrival of her niece.   She had
been talking of making a permanent home
at Trevlyn now that Monica was so utterly
alone, but her death stopped all such
schemes; and so it came about that in
absolute solitude the young widowed
countess took up her abode for the winter
in the great silent castle beside the sea.

The sea still exercised its old fascination
over Monica.   Her happiest hours were

spent wandering by its brink or riding along the breezy cliff. It was a friend indeed to her in those days, it frowned upon her no more. It had done its worst already —it had taken away the light of her life. Might it not be possible—was there not something of promise in its eternal music? Could it be that in some unexpected, mysterious way it would bring back some of the light that had been taken away— would be the means of uniting once again the hearts that had been so cruelly sundered? Strange thoughts and fancies flitted often through her brain, formless and indistinct, but comforting withal.

Returning to the castle at dusk one day, after one of these solitary rambles, she found an unusual bustle and excitement stirring there. Wilberforce hurried

forward to explain the cause of the un-
wonted tumult.

"I hope I have not done wrong, my
lady. You were not here to give orders,
and I could only act as I felt you would
wish. A lad came running in with a
scared face not half an hour back, saying
there was a man lying at the foot of the
cliffs, as if he had fallen over. I scarce
think he can be alive if that be so; but I
told the men that if he was—as there is no
other decent house near—I thought you
would wish——"

"That he should be brought here.
Quite right, Wilberforce. Is there a room
ready? Has Mr. l'endrill been sent for?"

"The groom has gone this twenty
minutes. Living or dead, he must have a
doctor to him. The maids are getting the

east room ready, yet I doubt if he can be living after such a fall."

" He may not have fallen over the cliff. He may have been scaling it, and have dropped from but a small height. See that everything likely to be needed is ready. He may be here almost immediately now."

She went up to the bed-room herself, to see if it were ready should there be need. It was probably only some poor tramp or fisherman who had met with the accident —no matter, he should be tended at Trevlyn, he should lie in its most comfortable guest-chamber, he should have every care that wealth could supply. Monica knew too well the dire results that might follow a slip down those hard, treacherous cliffs not to feel peculiarly tender and solicitous over another victim.

The steady tramp of feet ascending the
stairs and approaching the room where she
stood, roused Monica to the knowledge that
the injured man was not dead, and that
they were bringing him up to be tended
and nursed as she had directed. The door
was pushed open ; six men carried in their
burden upon an improvised stretcher, and
laid it just as it was upon the bed. Monica
stepped forward, and then started, growing
a little pale; for she recognised in the
death-like rigid face before her the well-
known countenance of Conrad Fitzgerald.

She could not look without a shudder at
that shattered frame, and Wilberforce
shook her head gravely, marvelling that
he yet breathed. None save professional
hands dared touch him, so distorted and
dislocated was every limb ; and yet by one

of those strange coincidences, not altogether uncommon in cases of accident, the beautiul face was entirely untouched, not marred by a scratch or contusion. Death-like unconsciousness had set its seal upon those chiselled, marble features, and had wiped from them every trace of passion or of vice.

Tom Pendrill was amongst them long before they looked for him. He had met the messenger not far from Trevlyn, and had come at once. He turned Monica out of the room with a stern precipitancy that perplexed her somewhat, as did also the expression of his face, which she did not understand. He shut himself up with his patient, retaining the services of Wilberforce and one of the men.

It was two hours before she saw him again.

37*

Monica wandered up and down the dark hall, revolving many things in her mind. What had brought Conrad so suddenly back at this melancholy time of the year? She had believed him abroad with his sister, with whom he seemed to have spent his time since his disappearance early in the spring. What had brought him back now? And why did he so haunt the frowning, treacherous cliffs of Trevlyn? Was he mad? But why did his madness always drive him to this spot? She asked many such questions of herself, but she could answer none of them.

At last Tom came down. His face looked as if carved in flint. She could not read the meaning of his glance.

"Is he dead?" she asked softly.

"He cannot last long. If he has any

relations near, they should be telegraphed for."

" His sister is in Italy, I believe. There is no one else that I know of."

" Then there is nothing to be done. He is sinking fast. He cannot live many hours. I doubt if he will last the night."

Monica's face was pale and grave.

" Poor Conrad!" she said, beneath her breath.

Tom started, and made a quick movement as of repulsion.

" No one could wish him to live," he began, almost roughly ; " he has hardly a whole bone in his body."

" Is he conscious ? "

" No, nor likely to be. It is not at all probable he will ever open his eyes again. He will most likely sink quietly, without a sound or a sign. I have done all I can for him. Somebody must be with him to watch him, I suppose. It can only be a question of hours now." A dark cloud hung upon the doctor's brow. His thoughts were pre-occupied. Presently he spoke again—a sort of mutter between his teeth.

"He ought not to be allowed to die here —under *this* roof. It is monstrous—hateful to think of! Nothing can save him. Yet I suppose it would be murder to move him now."

Monica looked up quickly.

"Move him! Tom, what are you thinking of?"

"I know it cannot be done," was the answer, spoken in a stern, dogged tone. "Yet I repeat what I said before : he ought not to be under this roof."

There was a gentle reproach in the look that Monica bent upon him.

"My husband's roof and mine will always be a refuge for any whose need is as sore as his. Sometimes I think, Tom, that you are the very hardest man I ever met. His life, I know, is terribly stained; yet it is not for us to judge him."

It seemed as if Tom were agitated. He gave no outward sign, but his face was pale, his manner curiously harsh and peremptory.

"You do not know," he said. "Your husband——"

She stopped him by a gesture.

"My husband would be the first to bid me return good for evil. You know Randolph very little if you do not know that. Conrad is dying, and death wipes out much.

He is about to answer for his life to a higher
tribunal than ours. Ah! let us not con-
demn him harshly. Have we not all our
sins upon our heads? When my turn
comes to answer for mine, let me not have
this one added—that I hardened my heart
against the dying, and denied the help and
succour mutely asked at the last hour."

"Monica," said Tom, with one of those
swift changes that marked his manner when
he was deeply moved, "were I worthy, I
would kiss the hem of your garment. As
it is, I can only say farewell. God be with
you!"

He was gone before she could open her
lips again. She stood in a sort of dream,
feeling as if some strange thing were about
to happen to her.

Night fell upon the castle and its inhabitants, but Monica could not sleep. If ever she closed her eyes in momentary slumber, the same vivid dream recurred again and again, till she was oppressed and exhausted by the effort to escape from it. It was Conrad, always Conrad, begging, praying, beseeching her to come. Sometimes it seemed as if his shadowy form stood beside her, wildly praying the same thing—to come to him—to come before it was too late.

At last she could stand it no longer. She rose and dressed. The clock in the tower struck four. She knew she could sleep no more that night. Why should she not take the watch beside the uncon-scious dying man, and let the faithful Wilberforce get some rest?

She stole noiselessly to the sick room. There had been no change in the patient's state. He lived, but could hardly live much longer. Wilberforce would fain have stayed, but Monica dismissed her quietly and firmly, preferring to keep her watch alone.

Profound silence reigned in the great house—silence only broken from time to time by the reverberating strokes of the clock in the tower, or by the sudden sinking of the coal in the grate and the quiet fall of the cinders. There was something inexpressibly solemn in the time, the place, and the office thus undertaken by Monica.

Conrad lay dying—Conrad, once her friend and playmate, then her bitterest, cruellest foe, now?—ah yes, what now?— she asked that question many times of herself. What strange, mysterious power is that of death! How it blots out all

hatred, anger, bitterness, and distrust, and
leaves in its place a sort of tender, mournful compassion. Who can look upon the
face of the dead, and cherish hard thoughts
of him that is gone ?

Not Monica, at least. Conrad had been
to her as the evil genius of one crisis of her
life—of more had she but known it. She
had said in her heart that she could never
forgive him, that she would never volun-
tarily look upon his face again, and yet
here he lay dying beneath her roof, and she
was with him. She could not, when it
came to the point, leave him to die alone,
with only a stranger beside him. He might
never know, his eyes would probably never
open to the light of this world again ; but she
should know, and in years to come, when
time should, even more than now, have

softened all things to her, she knew that
she should be glad to think she had shown
mercy and compassion towards one in death,
who had shown himself in life her bitterest
foe.

Very solemn thoughts filled her mind as
she sat in that quiet room, in which a strong
young life was quickly ebbing away. Would
the sin-stained soul pass into the shadowy
land of the hereafter in silence and darkness,
without one moment for preparation—perhaps for repentance? Would some slight
gleam of consciousness be granted? would
it be vouchsafed to him to wake once more
in this world, to give some sign to the
earnest, silent watcher whether he had tried
to make his peace with God before he was
called to his last account?

The lamp burned low—flickered in its

socket. That strange blue *film*, the first forerunner of the coming day, stole solemnly into that quiet room. Suddenly Monica became aware that Conrad's eyes were open, and fixed intently upon her face. She rose and stood beside him.

" You are here ? " he said, in a strange low voice. " I felt that you would hear me call — and would come. I knew I could not—die—till I had told you all."

She did not know how far he was conscious. His words were strange, but his eye was calm and quiet. He took the stimulant she held to his lips. It gave him an access of strength.

" Where am I ? " he asked.

" At Trevlyn."

A strange look flitted over his face.

" Ah! I remember now—I fell. And I

have been brought to Trevlyn—to die—
and you, Monica, are with me. It is
well."

She hardly knew what to say, or how to
answer the awed look in those dying
eyes. He bent a keen glance upon her.

"Will it be soon ?" he asked ; and she
knew that the "it" meant death. She
could not deceive him. She bent her head
in assent, as she said :

"Very soon, I think."

His eyes never left her face. His own
face moved not a muscle, but its expression
changed moment by moment in a way she
could not understand.

"There is not much time left, Monica.
Sit down by me where I can see you. I
must make a confession to you before I
die."

"Not to me, Conrad," said Monica gently. "Confess your sins to our Father in Heaven. He alone can grant forgiveness ; and His mercies are very great."

"Forgiveness!" the word was spoken with an intensity of bitterness that startled Monica. The horror was deepening each moment in his eyes. She began to feel that it was reflected in her own. What did it all mean?

"God is very merciful," she said gently, commanding herself so that he should not see her agitation.

"You do not know," he interrupted almost fiercely. "Wait till I have told you all."

"Why should you tell me, Conrad? I know much of your past life. I know that you have sinned. Ask God's forgiveness before it is too late. It is against Him, not me, that you have sinned."

"Against Him *and* you," he answered with a grave intensity of manner that plainly showed him master of his faculties. "Listen to me, Monica—you shall listen! I cannot carry the guilty secret to the grave. Death looks me in the face—he holds me by the hand, but he will not let me leave this world till I have told you all."

A sort of horror fell upon Monica. She neither spoke nor moved.

"Monica, turn your face this way. I want to see it. I must see it. You remember the night, a year ago, when—your husband—went away?"

She bent her head in silence.

"Did you know that I was there—in the boat with him?"

She raised her head, and looked at him speechlessly.

"I was there," he said, "but nobody knew, nobody suspected. I was on the shore before you. I saw you cling to him. I heard every word that passed. I think a demon entered into my soul as you kissed each other that night. 'Kiss her!' I said, 'kiss her—you shall never kiss her again!' Monica, I think sometimes I am mad—I was mad, possessed, that night. I had no will, no power to resist the evil spirit within me. He went down to the boat. I followed. In the black darkness nobody saw me swing myself in. You know the story the men told when they came back—it was all true enough. The crew of the sinking vessel had been rescued. Your husband left the boat to help the little lad.

I followed him, unknown to all. He had already handed the boy into the boat when I came stealthily up to him; the boat had swung round, and for a moment was lost in darkness before it could be brought up again. This was my chance. It was pitchy dark, and he did not see me, though I was close beside him. I had the great boat-hook in my hand; we were both sinking with the sinking vessel. I steadied myself, and brought the metal end of the weapon with all my strength upon his head. He sank without a cry. I saw his head, covered with blood, and his glassy eyes above the water for a moment—the sight has haunted me ever since—then I sprang into the boat. 'All right!' I shouted, and the men pulled off with a will, without a suspicion or a doubt. Almost before the boat reached the shore I sprang out, and vanished in the ·darkness before any one had seen me. My vow of vengeance was fulfilled. I murdered your husband Monica —do you understand?—I murdered him in cold blood! What have you to say to me?"

She sat still as a marble statue, her hands closely locked together. She spoke no word.

" I thought revenge would be sweet; but it has ·been bitter—bitter—bitter! I have known no peace night or day. I have been ceaselessly haunted by the sight of that ghastly·. face—ah, I see it now! Every time I lie down to sleep I am doomed to do that hideous deed again. 1 have fled time after time from the scene of my crime, only to be dragged back by

38*

a power I cannot resist. I knew that a terrible retribution would come; yet I could not keep away. And now—yes, it has come — more terrible than ever I pictured. I am dying—in his house—and you—his wife—are watching over me. Ah, it is frightful! Is there forgiveness with God for sin like mine? You say His mercies are great. Can they cover this hideous deed? Monica, can *you* forgive?"

He spoke with the wild, passionate appeal of despair. The anguish and remorse in his face were terrible to see; but Monica did not speak. She sat rigid and still, as pale as death, her eyes glowing like living fire in the wild conflict of her feelings. This was terrible—too terrible to be borne.

"Monica, I am dying — dying! The

shadows are closing round me. Ah, do not turn away! It is all so dark; if you desert me I am lost indeed! If you were dying you would understand. Monica, you say God is good—merciful. I have asked His pardon again and again for this black sin, and even as I pray it seems as if you — your pale, still face—rises ever between me and the forgiveness I crave. I read by this token that to you I must confess this blackest sin; of you I must ask pardon too. I have repented. I do repent. I would give my life to call him back. Monica, forgive—forgive! Have mercy upon a dying man. As you will one day ask pardon at God's hands even for your blameless life, give me your pardon ere I die!"

Who shall estimate the struggle that

raged in Monica's soul during the brief
moments that followed this appeal—
moments that to her were like hours, years,
for the concentrated passion of feeling that
surged through them? She felt as if she
had grown sensibly older, ere, white and
shaken by the conflict, she won the victory
over herself.

She rose and stood beside him.

"Conrad, I forgive you. May God
forgive you as I do."

A sudden light flashed into his dim eyes.
The awful, unspeakable horror passed slowly
away. The deep darkness lifted a little—a
very little—and Monica saw that it was so.

"I think—you have—saved me," he
whispered, whilst the death damp gathered
on his brow. "Monica, you will have your
reward for this—I know it—I feel it. Ah!

is this death? Monica—it is coming—
teach me to pray—I cannot—I have
forgotten—help me!"

"I will help you, Conrad. Say it after
me. 'Our Father which art in Heaven,
Hallowed be Thy name; Thy kingdom
come, Thy will be done on earth as it is in
Heaven; Give us this day our daily bread;
And forgive us our trespasses; As we
forgive'——"

"'As we forgive'——" Conrad broke
off suddenly; a strange look of gladness,
of relief, of comprehension, flashing over
the face that had been so full of terror and
anguish. "'As we forgive'—and you have
forgiven—then it may be that He will forgive too. I could not believe it before—now
I can—God be merciful to me, a sinner!"

Those were his last words. Already his

eyes were glazing. The hush as of the shadow of death was filling that dim room. Monica knelt beside the bed, a sense of deep awe upon her, praying with all the strength of her pure soul for the guilty, erring man—her husband's murderer—dying beneath his roof.

And as she thus knelt and prayed, a sudden sense of her husband's presence filled all her soul with an inexpressible, indescribable thrill of mingled rapture and awe. She trembled, and her heart beat thick and fast; whether she were in the spirit or out of the spirit she did not know. And then—in deep immeasurable distance, far, far away, and yet distinctly, sweetly clear—unmistakable—the sound of a voice —Randolph's voice—thrilling through infinity of space:

" Monica ! Monica ! My wife ! "

She started to her feet, quivering in every limb. Conrad's eyes were fixed upon her with an inexplicable look of joy. Had he heard it too ? What did it mean—that strange cry from the spirit world in this hour of death and dawn ?

She leant over the dying man.

" Conrad," she said, in a voice that was full of an emotion too deep for any but the simplest of words, " I forgive you—so does Randolph ; and I think God has forgiven you too."

The clear radiance of another day was shining upon the earth as the troubled, erring spirit was set free, and passed away into the great hereafter, whose secrets shall be read in God's good time, when all but His Word shall have passed away.

Let us not judge him—for is there not joy with the angels in heaven over one sinner that repenteth?

Yes, all was over now: all the weary warfare of sin and strife; and with a calm majesty in death, that the beautiful face had never worn in life, Conrad Fitzgerald lay dead in Castle Trevlyn.

CHAPTER THE THIRTIETH.

LORD HADDON.

"And you forgave him, Monica, you forgave him? The man who had killed your husband?"

It was Beatrice who spoke, and she spoke with a sort of horror in her tone. Tom stood a little apart in the recess of the window, a heavy cloud upon his brow. Lord Haddon was leaning with averted face upon the high carved mantel-shelf.

They had all come over early to Trevlyn to hear the fate of the hapless man who had died in the night. Beatrice felt an unquenchable longing to know if he had

spoken before he died—if by chance the
terrible secret had escaped in delirium from
his lips ; and she had insisted on coming
with her husband.   Her brother, who had
arrived unexpectedly the previous evening,
had made one of the party.   He was
hungering for another sight of Monica, and
Trevlyn seemed to draw him like a magnet.

Monica's face had told a tale of its own
when she had first appeared ; and the
whispered question on Beatrice's lips :

" Did he speak, Monica ?   Did he say
anything ? " elicited a reply that led to
explanations on both sides, rendering
further reserve needless ; and Monica told
her tale with the quiet calmness of one
who has too lately passed through some
great mental conflict to be easily disturbed
again.

But Beatrice, fiery, impetuous Beatrice, could not understand this calm. She was shaken by a tempest of excitement and wrath.

"You forgave him, Monica? Ah! how could you? Randolph's murderer!"

"Yes, I forgave him."

"You should not! You should not! It was not—it could not be right! Monica, I cannot understand you. I think you are made of stone!"

She said nothing; she smiled. That smile was only seen by Haddon. It thrilled him to his heart's core.

"How came you to be with him at all?" said Tom, almost sternly. "It was not your duty to be there. It was no fit place for you."

"I think my place is where there is

scrrow and need and loneliness," answered
Monica, very gently. "He needed me—
and I came to him."

"He sent for you?"

"I think he did."

"But you said——"

Monica lifted her hand; she rose to her
feet, passing her hand across her brow.

"You would not understand, dear.
There are some things, Beatrice, that you
are very slow to learn. You know something of the mysteries of life, but you do
not understand anything of those deeper
mysteries of death. I have forgiven a
dying man, who prayed forgiveness with
his latest breath—and you look at me with
horror."

Beatrice gazed at Monica, but yet would
not yield her point.

" Mercy can be carried too far——" but she could not say more, for the look upon Monica's face brought a sudden sense of choking that would have made her voice falter had she attempted to proceed. Her brother's murmured words, therefore, were now distinctly heard.

" Not in God's sight, perhaps."

Monica turned to him with a swift gesture inexpressibly sweet.

" Ah! you understand," she said simply. " I am glad you have come just now, Haddon. I shall want help. Will you give it me?"

" I will do anything for you, and esteem it an honour."

She looked at him steadily.

" Even if it is for one who—for the one who lies upstairs now—dead?"

Haddon bent his head.

"Even for him—at your bidding."

".Thank you," she said.

" I will take you home now, Beatrice," said Tom, curtly. " We are not wanted here."

Monica looked questioningly at him, as she gave him her hand, to see what this abruptness might signify. He returned her gaze with equal intensity.

" I believe you are an angel, Monica," he said, lifting her hand for a moment to his lips; " but there are moments when fallen mortals like ourselves feel the angelic presence a little overpowering."

Monica, as she had said, wanted the help of some man of business, as there was a good deal to be done in connection with

Conrad's sudden death: a good many trying formalities to be gone through, as well as much correspondence, and in Lord Haddon she found an able and willing assistant.

He saw much of Monica in those days. He was often at Trevlyn—hardly a day passed without his riding or driving across on some errand—and she was often at St. Maws herself, for Beatrice's momentary flash of anger had been rapidly quenched in deep contrition and humility; and both she and her husband treated Monica with the sort of reverential tenderness that seemed to meet her now on all hands.

Lord Haddon watched her day by day, wondering if ever he should dare to breathe a word of the hopes that filled his heart, reading in her calm face and

in the sisterly gentleness and fondness
with which she treated him, how little
conscious she was of the purpose that
possessed his soul. Sometimes he paused
and shrank from troubling the still waters
of their sweet, calm friendship, but then
again the thought of leaving her in her
loneliness and isolation seemed too sad and
mournful, if by any devotion and love he
could lighten the burden of her sorrow,
and bring back something of the lost
happiness into her life. Haddon was very
humble, very self-distrustful; he did not
expect to accomplish much, but he felt that
he would gladly lay down his life, if by
that act he could do anything to comfort
her. To die for her would, however, be
purposeless: the next thing was to try
and live for her.

And so one day, as they paced the lonely shore together, on a chill cloudy winter's afternoon, he put his fate to the touch.

She had noticed his silence—his abstraction: he had not been quite himself all day. Presently they reached a sheltered nook amongst some rocks not far from the water's edge, and she sat down, motioning him to do the same. She looked at him with gentle, friendly concern.

" Is anything the matter?" she asked. " Have you something on your mind ? "

He turned his head, looked into her eyes, and answered:

" Yes."

" Can I help you?" she continued, in the same sweet way. " You help me so often, that it is my turn to help you now if I can."

39*

He looked with a glance she could not altogether understand.

" Monica," he said, " may I speak to you ?—may I tell you something ? I have tried to do so before, and have failed; but I ought not to go on longer without speaking. Have I your permission to tell you what is on my mind? "

He did not often call her by her Christian name : only in moments of excitement, when his soul was stirred within him. The unconscious way in which it dropped now from his lips told that he was deeply moved. A sort of vague uneasiness arose within her, but she looked into his troubled, resolute face, and answered :

" Tell me if you wish it, Haddon "— although she shrank, without knowing why, from the confession she was to hear.

" Monica," he said, not looking at her, but out over the sea, and speaking with a manly resolution and fluency unusual with him, the outcome of a very earnest purpose, " I am going to speak to you at last, and I must ask you beforehand to pardon my presumption, of which I am as well aware as you can ever be. Monica, I think that no woman in the wide world is like you. I have thought so ever since I saw you first, in your bridal robes, standing beside Randolph in that little church over yonder. When I saw you then—nay, pardon me if I pain you; I should not have recalled the memory, and yet I cannot help it— I said within myself that you were one to be worshipped with the truest devotion of a man's heart; and the more I saw of you in later life, the deeper did that

feeling sink into my soul. He, your husband, had been as a brother to me, and to
feel that I was thus brought near to you,
admitted to friendship and to confidence,
was a source of keen pleasure such as I
can ill describe. You did not know your
power over me, Monica. I hardly knew it
myself; but I think I would at any time
have laid down my life either for him or
for you. I know I would that fatal night
—but I must not pain you more. When
I awoke, Monica, from that long fever, to
find you watching beside me, to hear that
he, my friend, was dead, and you left all
alone in your desolation—Monica, Monica,
how can I hope to express to you what I
felt? It is not treachery to his memory—
believe me, it is not. If I could call him
back, ah! how gladly would I do it!—at

the cost of my life if need be—but that can never, never be ! I know I can never fill *his* place. I know I am utterly unworthy of the boon I ask ; but if a life-long devotion, if a love that will never change nor falter, if the ceaseless care of one, who is yours wholly and entirely, can ever help to fill the blank, can in ever so small a degree make up to you for that one irretrievable loss, believe me, it will be the greatest happiness I can ever know. Monica, need I say more? Have I said too much? I only ask leave to watch over you, to comfort you, to love you ; I ask nothing for myself—only the right to do this. Can you not give it to me? God helping me, you shall never repent it if you do."

A long pause followed this confession—

this appeal. Monica's face had expressed
many fluctuating feelings as he had proceeded with his speech. Now it was full
of a sort of divine compassion and tenderness: a look sometimes seen in a pictured saint or Madonna drawn by a master
hand.

"You are so good," she said, very low;
"so very, very good; and it grieves me so
sadly to give you pain."

He turned his head and looked at her.
His eyes darkened with sudden sorrow.

"I have spoken too soon," he said, in
the same gentle, self-contained way. "I
have tried to be patient, but seeing you
lonely and sad makes it so hard. I
should have waited longer—it is only a
year now since. Monica, do not think me
hard or callous to say it, but time is a

great softener—a great healer. I do not mean that you will ever forget; but years will go by, and you are still quite young, very young to live your life always alone. Think of the years that lie before you. Must they all be spent alone? Monica, do not answer me yet; but if in time to come —if you want a friend, a helper—let me —can you think of me? Ah! how can I say it? Can I ever be more to you than I am now? You understand: you have only to call me, to command me—I will come."

He spoke with some agitation now, but it was quickly subdued. It seemed as if he would have left her, but she laid her hand upon his arm and detained him.

"Haddon," she said, softly, " I am lonely and I do want a friend. You have been a friend to me always; I trust and love you as a brother. May I not do so always? Can you not be content with that? Must it end with us, that love and trust? I should miss it sorely if it were withdrawn."

Her sweet, pleading face was turned towards him. There was a sort of struggle in the young man's mind : then he answered quietly :

"It shall be so, if you wish it," he said. "My chiefest wish is for your happiness. But——"

She checked him by a look.

"Haddon, I am Randolph's wife!"

His eyes gave the reply his tongue would never have uttered. She answered as if he had spoken.

"Yes, he is dead. Did you think that

made any difference? Ah, you do not understand. When I gave myself to Randolph, I gave myself for ever—not for a time only but for always. He is my husband. I am his wife. Nothing can change that."

" Not even death?"

The words were a mere whisper; yet she heard them. It seemed as if a sudden ray of light shone upon the face she turned towards him. He was awed; he watched her in mute silence.

" Ah! no," she said, very softly, "not death—death least of all. Death can only divide us, it cannot touch our love. Ah! you do not know, you do not understand. How can I make it clear to you? Love is like nothing else in the world—it is us, our very selves. *Somewhere*—— " Monica clasped her hands together, and stretched them out before her towards the eternal ocean, with a gesture more eloquent than any words, whilst the light upon her face deepened in intensity every moment as her eyes fixed themselves upon the far horizon. "*Somewhere* he is waiting for me to come to him—he, my husband, my love; and though he may not come back to me, I shall go to him in God's good time, and when I join him in the great, eternal home, I must go to him as he left me—with nothing between us and our love; and there will be no parting there, no more death, and no more sea."

Her words died away in silence; but her parted lips, her shining eyes, the light upon her face, spoke an eloquent language of their own. Her companion sat and looked

at her in mute, breathless silence, not un-
mixed with awe.

He knew his cause was lost. He knew
she could never, never be his; yet, strange
to say, he was not saddened or cast down,
for by this revelation of her innermost
heart he felt himself uplifted and ennobled.
His idol was not shattered. Monica was,
as ever, enshrined in his heart—the one
ideal woman to be worshipped, reverenced,
adored. Even in this supreme hour of his
life, when the airy fabric of his dreams was
crumbling into dust about him, he had a
perception that perhaps even thus it was
best. He never could be worthy of
her, and now he might still call himself
her friend; had she not said so herself?

There was a long, long silence between
them. Then he moved, kneeling on one

knee before her, and taking her hand in his.

"Monica," he said, "I understand now. I shall never trouble you again. You have judged well, very well; it is like you, and that is enough. But before I go may I crave one boon?"

"And that is——?"

"That you forget all that I have said, all the wild, foolish words that I have spoken; and let me keep my old place—as your brother and friend."

She looked at him with her own gentle smile.

"I wish for nothing better," she answered. "I cannot afford to lose my friend."

He pressed her hand for one moment to his lips, and was gone without another word.

Tears slowly welled up in Monica's eyes as she rose at last, and stood looking out over the vast waste of heaving grey sea—sad, colourless, troubled.

"Like my life," she said softly to herself. And yet she had just put away a love that might at least have cast a glow upon it, and gilded its dim edges.

She stretched out her hand with a sort of mute gesture of entreaty.

"Ah! Randolph, husband, come back to me! I am so lonely, so desolate!"

Even as she spoke, the setting sun, as it touched the horizon, broke through the bank of cloud which had veiled it all the day, and flooded the sea as with liquid gold—that cold grey sea that she had just been likening to her own future life.

She could not help an involuntary start.

"Is it an omen?" she asked; and despite the heavy load at her heart, she went home somewhat comforted.

CHAPTER THE THIRTY-FIRST.

CHRISTMAS.

IT was Christmas Eve; the light was just beginning to wane, and Monica's work was done at last. She was free now until the arrival of her guests—the Pendrills and Lord Haddon—should give her new occupation in hospitable care for them.

Monica had been too busy for thoughts of self to intrude often upon her during these past days. She wished to be busy; she tried to occupy herself from morning to night, for she found that the aching hunger of her heart was more eased by loving deeds of mercy and kindness than

in any other way—self more fully lost in
ceaseless care for others. But when all
was done, every single thing disposed of,
nothing more left to think of or to accomplish; then the inevitable reaction set in,
and with a heart aching to pain, almost to
despair, Monica entered the music-room,
and sat down to her organ.

She played with a sort of passionate
appeal that was infinitely pathetic, had any
one been there to hear; she threw all the
yearning sadness of her soul into her
organ, and it seemed to answer her back
with a promise of strong sympathy and
consolation. Insensibly she was soothed
by the sweet sounds she evoked. She fell
into a dreamy mood, playing softly in a
minor key, so softly that through the door
that stood ·ajar, she became aware of a

slight subdued tumult in the hall without, to which she gave but a dreamy attention at first.

The bell had pealed sharply, steps had crossed the hall, the door had been opened, and then had followed the tumultuous sounds expressive of astonishment that roused Monica from her dreamy reverie. She supposed the party from St. Maws had arrived somewhat before the expected time, and rose, and had made a few steps forward when she suddenly stopped short and stood motionless—spell-bound—what was it she had heard?—only the sound of a voice—a man's voice.

"Where is your mistress?"

The words were uttered in a clear, deep, ringing tone, that seemed to her to waken every echo in the castle into wild

40*

surging life. The very air throbbed and palpitated around her—her temples seemed as if they would burst. What was the meaning of that sound—that wild tumult of voices? Why did she stand as if carved in stone, growing white to the very lips, whilst thrill upon thrill ran through her frame, and her heart beat to suffocation? What did it all portend? Whose was the voice she had just heard—that voice from the dead? *Who* was it that stood in the hall without?

The door was flung open. A tall, dark figure stood in the dim light.

" Monica ! "

Monica neither spoke nor moved. The cry of awe and of rapture that rose from her heart could not find voice in which to utter itself—but what matter? She was in her husband's arms. Her head lay upon his breast. His lips were pressed to her cold face in the kisses she had never thought to feel again. Randolph had come back. She could not speak. She had no will to try and frame a single word. He held her in his arms; he strained her ever closer and closer. She felt the tumultuous beating of his heart as she lay in his arms, powerless to move or think. She heard his murmured words, broken and hoarse with the passionate feeling of that supreme moment.

"My wife! Monica! My wife!"

And then for a time she knew no more. Sight and hearing alike failed her; it seemed as if a slumber from heaven itself sealed her eyes and stole away her senses.

When she came to herself she was on a sofa in her own room, and Randolph was

kneeling beside her.   She did not start to
see him there.   For a moment it seemed as
if he had never left her.   She smiled her
own sweet smile.

"Randolph!   Have I been asleep—
dreaming?"

He took her hands in his, and bent to
kiss her lips.

"It has been a long dream, my Monica,
and a dark one; but it is over at last.
My darling, my darling!   God grant I
may not be dreaming now!"

She smiled like a tired child.   She had a
perception that something overpoweringly
strange and sudden had happened, but she
did not want to rouse herself just yet to
think what it must all mean.

Two hours later, in the great drawing-room ablaze with light, Monica and Randolph stood together to welcome their guests. She had laid aside her mournful widow's garb, and was arrayed in her shimmering bridal robes. Ah, how lovely she was in her husband's eyes as she stood beside him now! Perhaps never in all her life had she looked more exquisitely fair. Happiness had lighted her beautiful eyes, and had brought the rose back to her pale cheeks: she was glorified—transfigured— a vision of radiant beauty.

He had changed but slightly during his mysterious year of absence. There were a few lines upon his face that had not been there of old: he looked like a man who had been through some ordeal, whether mental or physical it would be less easy to tell; but the same joy and rapture that emanated, as it were, from Monica was reflected in his face likewise, and only a keen eye could read to-night the traces of pain or of sorrow in that strong, proud, manly countenance.

Monica looked at him suddenly, the flush deepening in her cheeks.

"Hush! They are coming!" she said, and waited breathlessly.

The door opened, admitting Mrs. Pendrill, Beatrice, and Tom. There was a pause—a brief, intense silence, during which the fall of a pin might have been heard, and then, with one long, low cry, half-sobbing, half-laughing, Beatrice rushed across the room, and flung herself upon Randolph.

Monica went straight up to Mrs. Pendrill, and put her arms about her neck.

" Aunt Elizabeth, he has come home,"

she said, in a voice that shook a little with the tumult of her happiness. "He has just come home—this very day—Randolph— my husband. Help me to believe it. You must help me to bear this—as you helped me to bear the other."

Tom had by this time grasped Randolph by the hand ; but neither trusted his own voice. They were glad that Beatrice covered their silence by her incoherent exclamations of rapture, and by the flow of questions no one attempted to answer.

It was all too like a dream for anyone to recollect very clearly what happened. Raymond and Haddon came in almost at once, new greetings had to be gone through. How the dinner passed off that night no one afterwards remembered. There was a deep sense of thankfulness and joy in every heart; yet of words there were few. But when gathered round the fire later on in the evening, when they had grown used to the presence amongst them of one whom they had mourned as dead for more than a year, Randolph was called upon to tell his tale, which was listened to in breathless silence.

"I will tell you all I can about it; but there are points yet where my memory fails me, where I have but little idea what happened. I have a dim recollection of the night of the wreck, and of leaving the boat; but I must have received a heavy blow on the head, the doctors tell me, and I suppose I sank, and the men could not find me. But I was entangled, it seems, in the rigging of a floating spar, and must have been carried thus many miles ; for I was picked up by an ocean steamer bound for Australia, which had been driven somewhat out of its course by the gale. It was not supposed that I could live after so many hours' exposure. I was quite unconscious, and remained so for a very long time. There was nothing upon me by which I could be identified, and of course I could give no account of myself. On board the boat were a kind-hearted wealthy Australian couple, who had lately lost an only son, to whom they fancied I bore some slight resemblance. Perhaps for this cause, perhaps from true kindness of heart, they at once took me under their special care and protection. There was plenty of space on board the vessel, and they looked after me as if I had indeed been their son. They would not hear of my being left behind in hospital on the way out. They took me under their protection until I should be able to give an account of myself.

"Of course I knew nothing about all this. I was lying dangerously ill of brain fever all the while, not knowing where I was, or what was happening. When we reached Melbourne at last, and I was conveyed to their luxurious house on the outskirts of the town, I was still in the same state, relapse following relapse, every time till I gained a little ground, till for months my life was despaired of. I was either raving in delirium, or lying in a sort of unconscious stupor, and without all the skill and care lavished upon me, I suppose I must have died. But I did not die. Gradually, very gradually, the fever abated, and I began to come to myself: that is to say, I began to know the faces around me and to recognise my surroundings; but for myself, I knew no more who I was, nor whence I had come, than the infant just born into the world. My memory had gone, had been wiped clean away; I had no idea of my own identity, no recollection of the past. The very effort to remember brought on such pain and distress that I was imperatively commanded to relinquish the attempt. Gradually some things came back to my mind: I could read, write, understand the foreign tongues I had mastered, and the sciences I had studied in past days. As my health slowly improved this kind of knowledge came back spontaneously and without effort; but my personal history was as a blank wall, against which I flung myself in vain. It would yield to no efforts of mine. Distressed and confused, I was obliged to give up, and wait with what patience I might for the realisation of the hope held out cheerfully by the clever doctor who attended me. He maintained that if I would but have patience, some strong association of ideas would some day bring all back in a flash, and meantime all I had to do was to get strong and well, so as to be ready for action when that day should come. I was restless sometimes, but less so than one would fancy, for the blank was too complete to be distressing. My good friends and protectors were unspeakably kind and good, and did everything in their power to ensure my mental and physical well-being; I recovered my health rapidly, soon my memory was to come back too."

Randolph passed his hand across his eyes. No one spoke, every eye was fixed upon his face.

" It did so very strangely: it was one hot afternoon in November—our summer, you know "—he named the date and the hour, and Monica heard it with a sudden thrill. Allowing for the discrepancy of time, it was during the moments that she watched by Conrad Fitzgerald's dying bed that her husband's memory was given back to him.

" I was looking over some old English newspapers, idly, purposelessly, when I came upon a detailed account of the wreck, and of my own supposed death. As I read —I cannot describe what it was like—my

memory came back to me in a great
flood, like overwhelming waves. It seemed,
Monica, as if my spirit were carried on
wings to Trevlyn, as if I were hovering over
you in some mysterious way impossible to
describe. I called your name aloud. I knew
that I was close to you, at Trevlyn—it is
useless to attempt to define what I felt.
When I came to myself they told me I had
fainted ; but that was not so. I had been
on a journey, that is all, and had returned.
My memory was restored from that hour,
clearly and distinctly ; the doctor thought
there might be lapses, that I might never
be the same man again as I had been once ;
but I have felt no ill effects since. Little
more remains to be told. My first instinct
was to telegraph ; but not knowing what
had happened in my absence, knowing I

must long have been given up for lost, I was afraid to do so, lest hopeless confusion should result. Instead, I took the first home-bound steamer, and reached London late last night. I found out at the house there where Monica was, and came on here by the first train. I have come back home to spend my Christmas with you."

CHAPTER THE THIRTY-SECOND.

THE LAST.

"Monica, I could not tell you last night— it was all so sudden, so wonderful—but I think you know, without any words of mine, how glad, how thankful, I am."

It was Haddon who spoke, spoke with a glad, frank, joyous sincerity, that beamed in his eye and sounded in every tone of his voice. Monica gave him both her hands, looking up into his face with her sweetest smile.

"I know, Haddon; I know. I am sure of it. Is he not almost a brother to you?—and are you not the best of brothers to me?"

" At least I will try to be," he answered gladly. " I cannot tell you how happy this has made me."

She was glad, too: glad to see him so happy, so heart-whole. He had loved her with the loyal love of a devoted chivalrous knight, had loved her for her sorrow and her loneliness; but she was comforted now, and he was able to rejoice with her. It was all very good—just as she would have it.

Ah! what a day of joy and thanksgiving it was! How Monica's heart beat as she knelt by her husband's side that glad Christmas morning in the little cliff church, when, in the pause just before the General Thanksgiving, the grey-headed clergyman, with a little quiver in his voice, announced that Randolph Trevlyn desired to return thanks to Almighty God for preservation from great perils, and for restoration to his home.

Her voice faltered in the familiar words, and many suppressed sobs were heard in the little building, but they were sobs of joy and gratitude, and tears of healing and of happiness stole down Monica's cheeks. It was like some beautiful dream, and yet too sweet not to be true.

In the afternoon Monica and Randolph went out alone together ; first into the whispering pine woods, and then out upon the breezy cliff, hard beneath their feet with the winter's frost.

He let her lead him whither she would. He had no thought to spare for aught beside herself. They were together once again. What more could they need ?

But Monica had an object in view ; and

as they walked, engrossed in each other, in sweet communion of soul and interchange of thought, or the almost sweeter silence of perfect peace and tranquillity, she led him once more towards the little cliff church; though only when she was unlatching the gate to enter the quiet grave-yard did he arouse to the sense of their surroundings.

" Why, Monica," he said, " why have you brought me here ? We are too late for service."

" I know," she answered ; " but come. I want to show you something."

Her face wore an expression he did not understand. He followed her in silence to a secluded corner, where, beneath a dark yew tree, stood a green mound, at the head of which a wooden cross had been temporarily erected.

Randolph read the letters it bore :

" C. F.," followed by a date, and beneath, the simple, familiar words —

" *Requiescat in pace.*"

Strange, perhaps, that Monica should have cared for this lonely grave, in which was laid to rest one who had, as she believed, robbed her life of all its brightness and joy. Strange that she, in the absence of friend or kinsman, should have charged herself with keeping it, and of erecting there some monument to mark who lay there low. Strange—yet so it was.

Her husband looked at her questioningly.

" Conrad's grave — yes," she answered quietly. " Randolph, look at the date."

He did so, and started a little.

" He died at dawn that day, Randolph.

You know what was happening then at the other side of the world?"

There was a strange look of awe upon her face as she spoke, which was reflected in his also. She came and stood close beside him.

"Randolph, do you know that he was there—that night?—that he tried to kill you?"

He had taken off his hat as he stood beside the grave, with the instinctive reverence for the dead—even though it be a dead foe—characteristic of a noble mind. Now he passed his hand across his brow and through his thick dark hair.

"I thought that was a delusion of fever—a sort of hideous vision founded on no reality. Monica, was it so?"

"It was."

"How do you know?"

"I had it from his own lips."

He gazed at her without speaking; something in her face awed and silenced him.

"Randolph, listen," she said. "I must tell you all. Six weeks ago, the evening before *that* day, he was brought, shattered and dying, to Trevlyn; he had fallen from the cliffs, no skill could serve to prolong his life. I knew nothing then—he was profoundly unconscious, yet as the night wore away some strange intuition came upon me that he wanted me, that he was beseeching me to come to him. I went— he was still unconscious. I sent Wilberforce away and watched by him myself. Randolph, at dawn he awoke to consciousness—he told me all his awful tale—he said he had murdered you—I believed it was true. He was dying—dying in darkness and in dread, and he prayed for my forgiveness as if his salvation hung upon it. Randolph, Randolph, how can I tell you?—I cannot, no I cannot—no one could understand," for a moment she pressed her hand upon her eyes, looking up again in a few seconds with a calm glance that was like a smile. "He was dying, Randolph, and I forgave him—I forgave him freely and fully—and he died in peace. Stop, that is not all. Randolph, as I knelt beside his bed, praying for the sin-stained spirit then taking its flight, I felt that you were with me; I had never before felt the strange overshadowing presence that I did then— you were there, your own self. I heard your voice far away, yet absolutely clear, like a call from some distant, snow-clad mountain-top, infinitely far — 'Monica! Monica! My wife!' I think Conrad heard it too, for he died with a smile on his lips. Randolph, I am sure that you were with me in that strange, awful hour. I knew it then—I know it better now. Randolph, I think that love is stronger than all else—time, space, death itself. Nothing touched our love. I think it is like eternity.".

A deep look of awe had stamped itself upon Randolph's face. He put his arm round Monica, and for a very long while they stood thus, neither attempting to speak or to move.

At last he woke from his reverie, and looked down at her with a strange light shining in his eyes.

" And you forgave him, Monica?"

She looked up and met his gaze unfalteringly.

"I forgave him, Randolph ; was I wrong?"

He stooped and kissed her.

"My wife, I thank God that you did forgive him. His life was full of sin and sorrow—but at least its end was peace. May God pardon him as you did—as I do."

There was a strange sweet smile in her eyes as she lifted them to his.

"Ah, Randolph!" she said softly, "I knew you would understand. Oh, my husband, my husband!"

He held her in his arms, and she looked up at him with a sweet, tender smile. Then her eyes wandered dreamily out over the wide sea beneath them.

"There is nothing sad there now, Randolph. It will never separate us again."

He looked down at her with a world of love in his eyes; yet as they turned away his glance rested for one moment upon the lonely grave he had been brought to see, and lifting his hat once more, he murmured beneath his breath—"Requiescat in pace."

Then drawing his wife's hand within his arm, he led her homewards to Trevlyn, whilst the sun set in a blaze of golden glory over the boundless shining sea.

THE END.

www.ingramcontent.com/pod-product-compliance
Lightning Source LLC
Chambersburg PA
CBHW020612030726
47497CB00007B/2197